Bolton
Council

Please return/renew this item
by the last date shown.
Books may also be renewed by
phone or the Internet.

HW

Tel: 01204 332384
www.bolton.gov.uk/libraries

Raintree is an imprint of Capstone Global Library Limited, a
company incorporated in England and Wales having its registered
offi ce at 7 Pilgrim Street, London, EC4V 6LB - Registered company
number: 6695582

www.raintree.co.uk
myorders@raintree.co.uk

Text © Capstone Global Library Limited 2015

Printed and bound in China

ISBN 978 1 4062 7990 0
18 17 16 15 14
10 9 8 7 6 5 4 3 2 1

British Library Cataloguing in Publication Data
A full catalogue record for this book is available from the British
Library.

All the internet addresses (URLs) given in this book were valid at
the time of going to press. However, due to the dynamic nature
of the internet, some addresses may have changed, or sites may
have changed or ceased to exist since publication. While the author
and publisher regret any inconvenience this may cause readers, no
responsibility for any such changes can be accepted by either the
author or the publisher.

Mighty Mighty **MONSTERS**

THE GREMLIN'S CURSE

created by
Sean O'Reilly

illustrated by
Arcana Studio

In a strange corner of the world known as Transylmania . . .

Legendary monsters were born.

WELCOME TO TRANSYLMANIA

But long before their frightful fame, these classic creatures faced fears of their own.

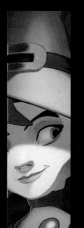

To take on terrifying teachers and homework horrors, they formed the most fearsome friendship on Earth . . .

Mighty Mighty MONSTERS

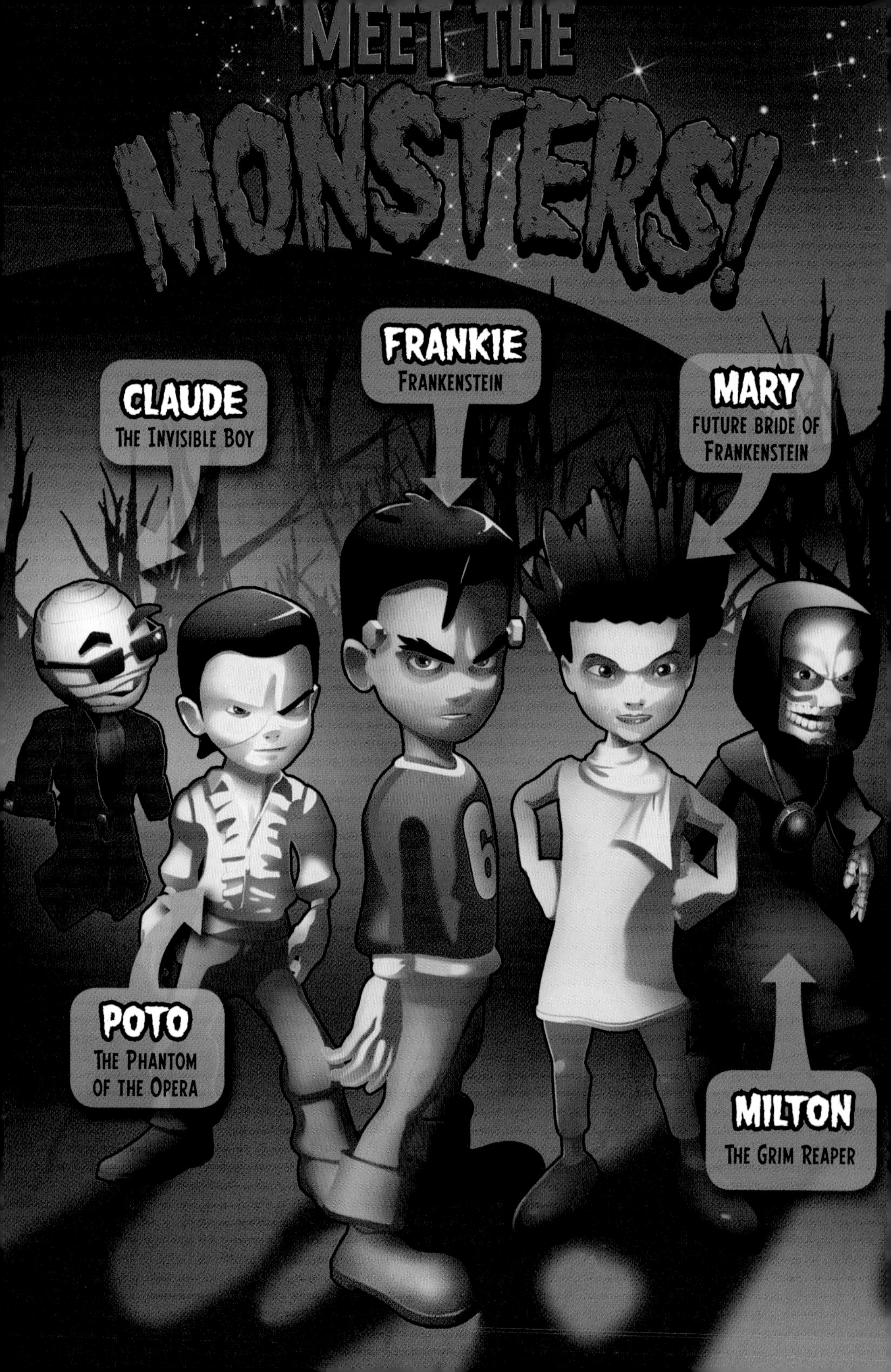
MEET THE MONSTERS!
FRANKIE
FRANKENSTEIN
CLAUDE
THE INVISIBLE BOY
MARY
FUTURE BRIDE OF FRANKENSTEIN
POTO
THE PHANTOM OF THE OPERA
MILTON
THE GRIM REAPER

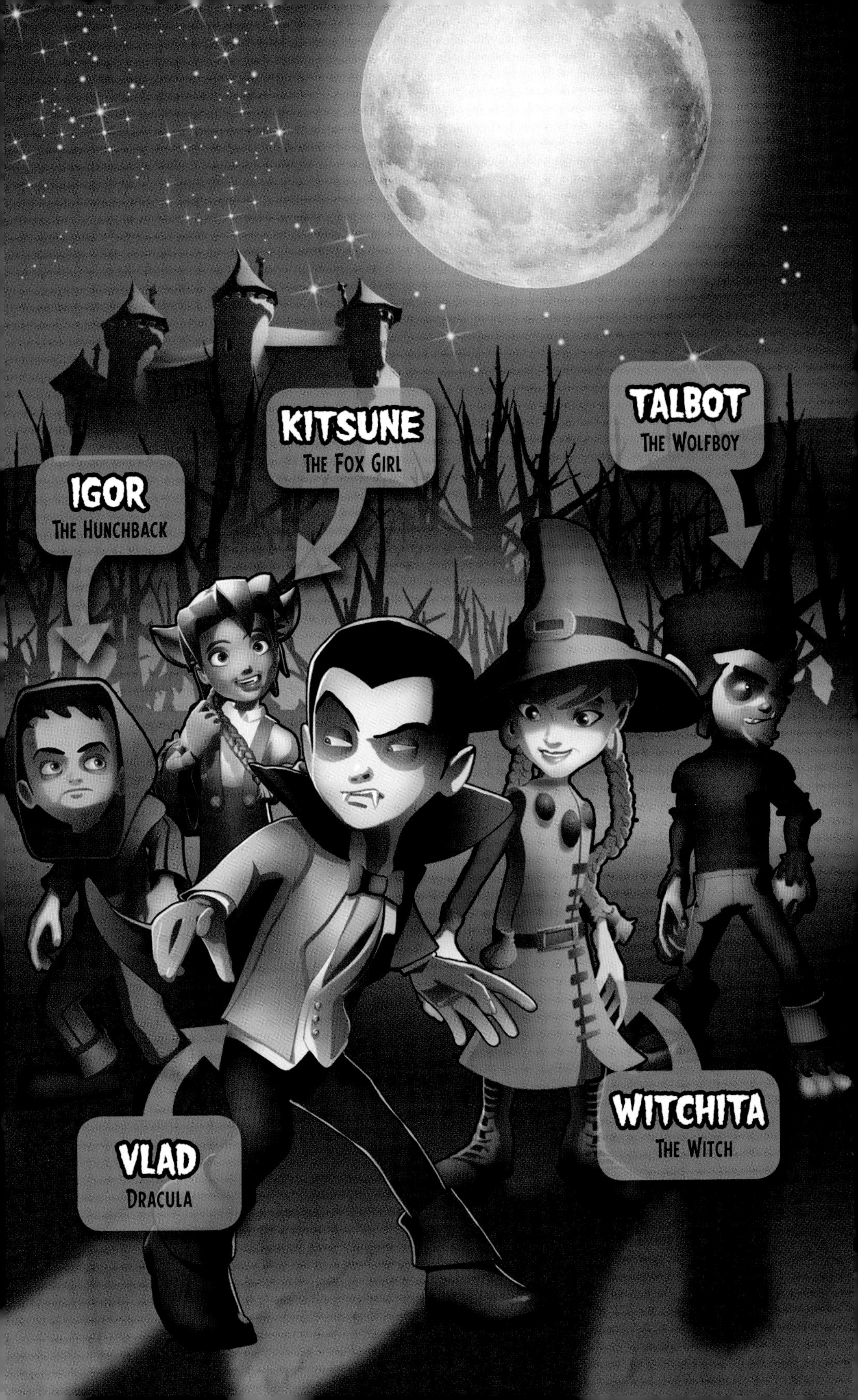
KITSUNE
THE FOX GIRL
TALBOT
THE WOLFBOY
IGOR
THE HUNCHBACK
VLAD
DRACULA
WITCHITA
THE WITCH

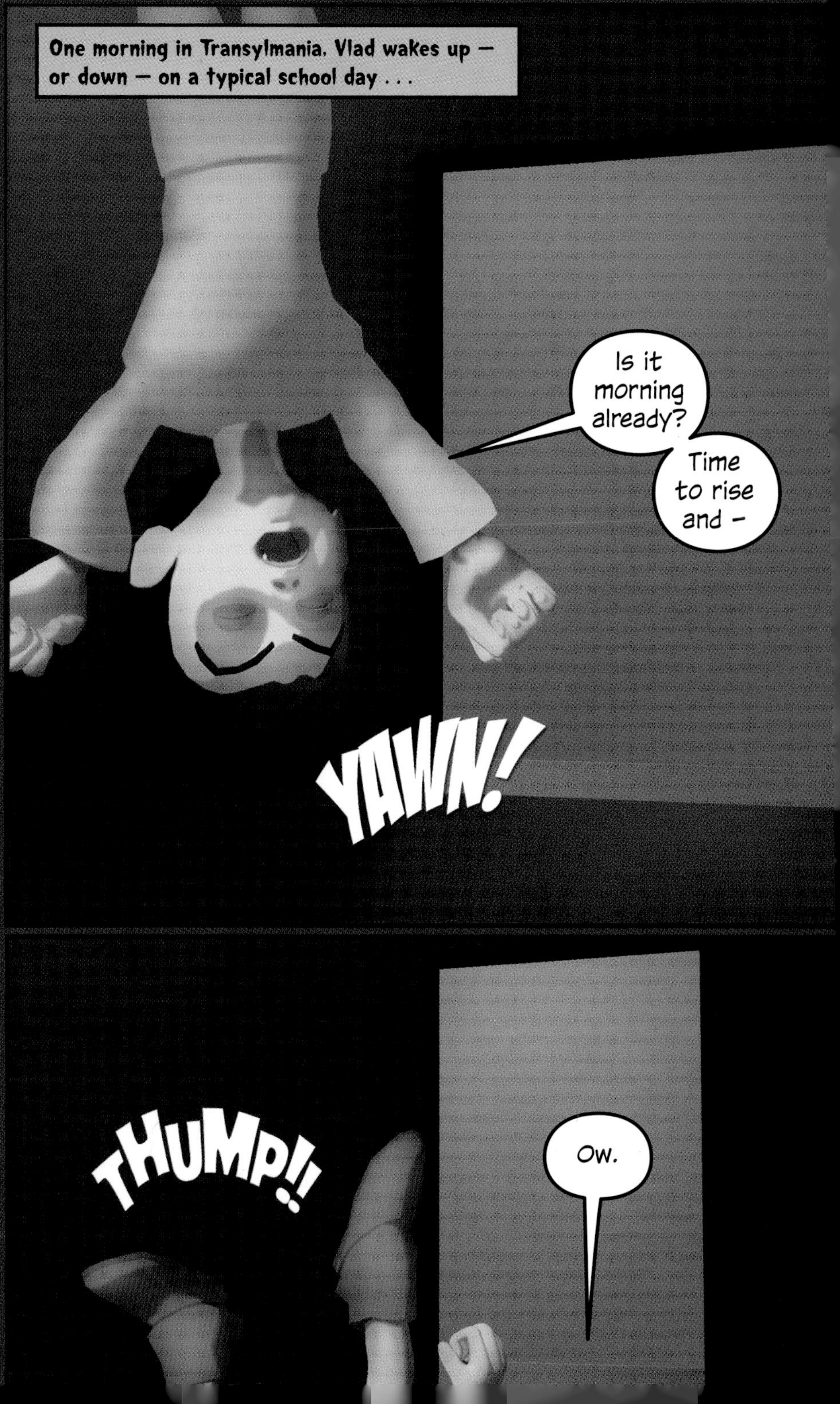
One morning in Transylmania, Vlad wakes up — or down — on a typical school day . . .
Is it morning already?
Time to rise and –
YAWN!
THUMP!!
Ow.

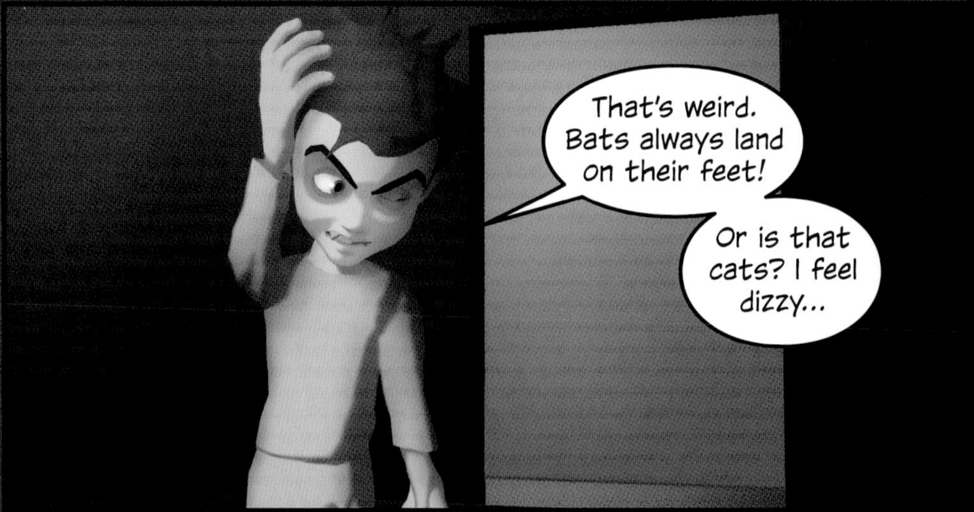
That's weird. Bats always land on their feet!
Or is that cats? I feel dizzy...

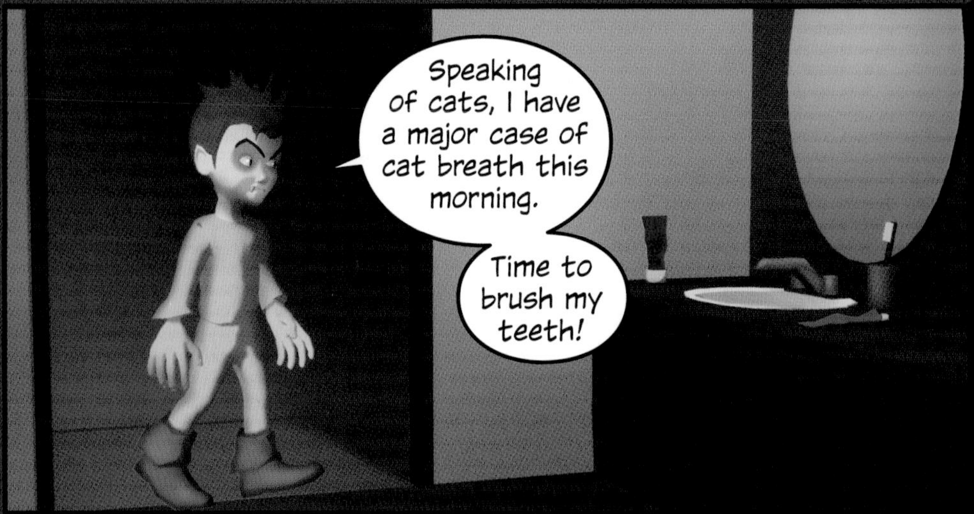
Speaking of cats, I have a major case of cat breath this morning.
Time to brush my teeth!

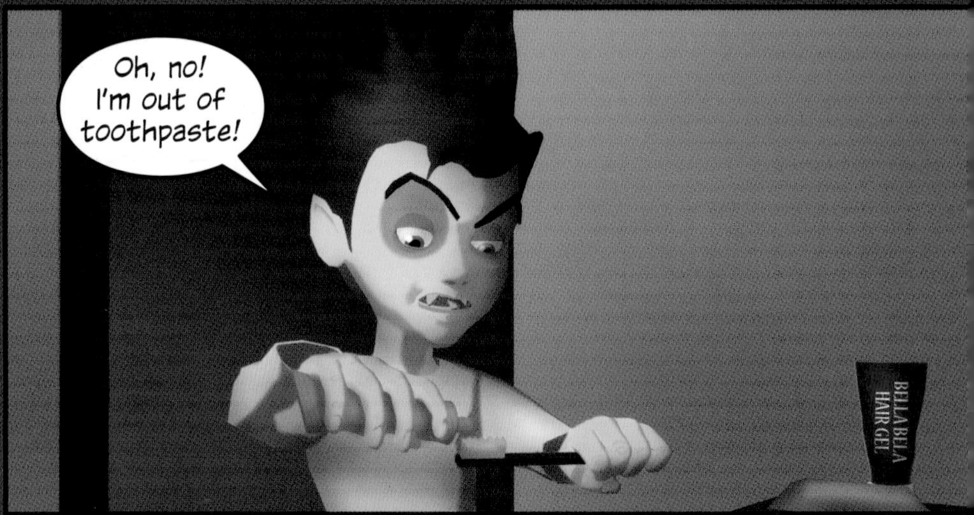
Oh, no! I'm out of toothpaste!
BELLA BELLA HAIR GEL

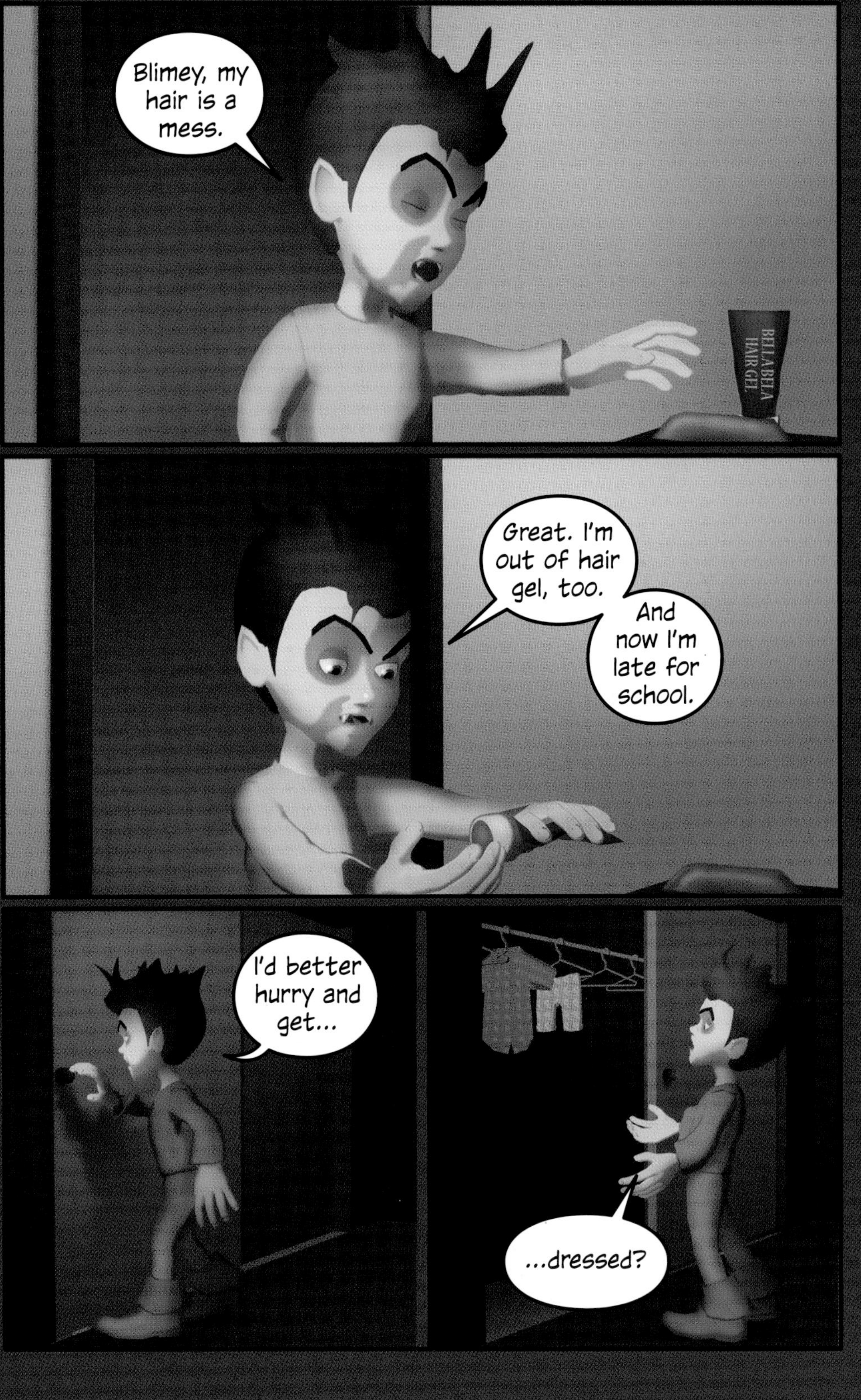
Blimey, my hair is a mess.
BELLA BELA HAIR GEL
Great. I'm out of hair gel, too.
And now I'm late for school.
I'd better hurry and get...
...dressed?

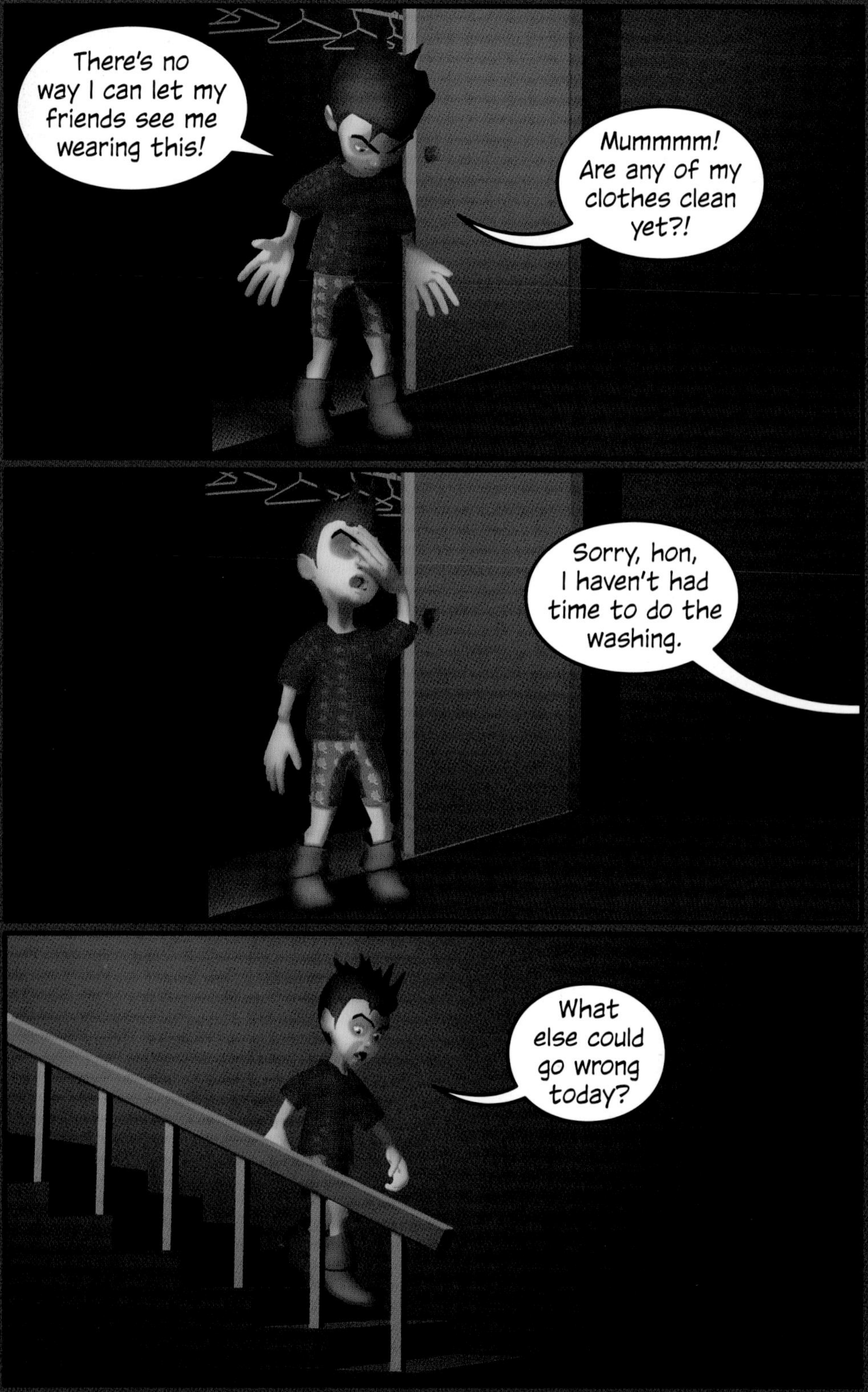
There's no way I can let my friends see me wearing this!
Mummmm! Are any of my clothes clean yet?!
Sorry, hon, I haven't had time to do the washing.
What else could go wrong today?

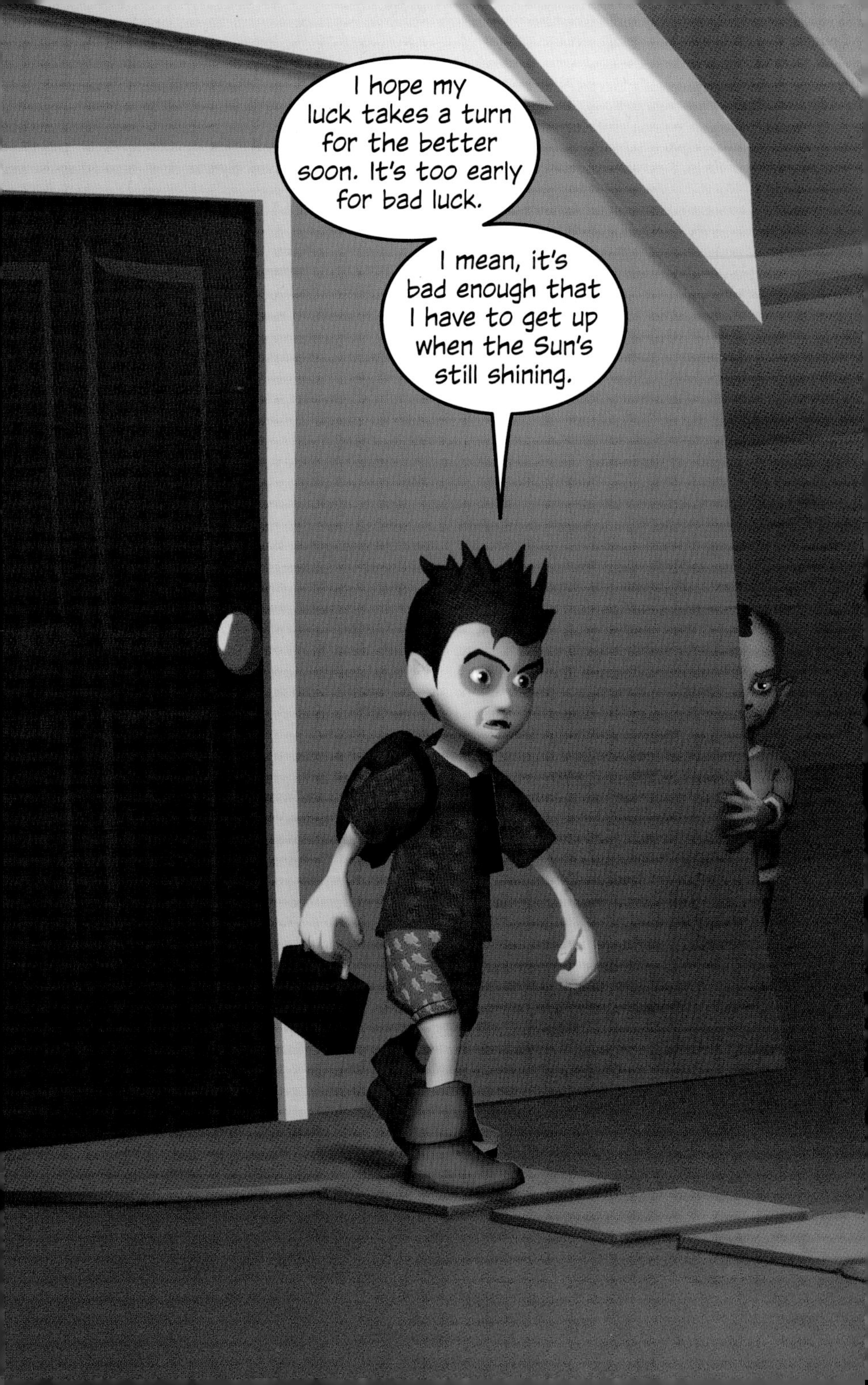
I hope my luck takes a turn for the better soon. It's too early for bad luck.
I mean, it's bad enough that I have to get up when the Sun's still shining.

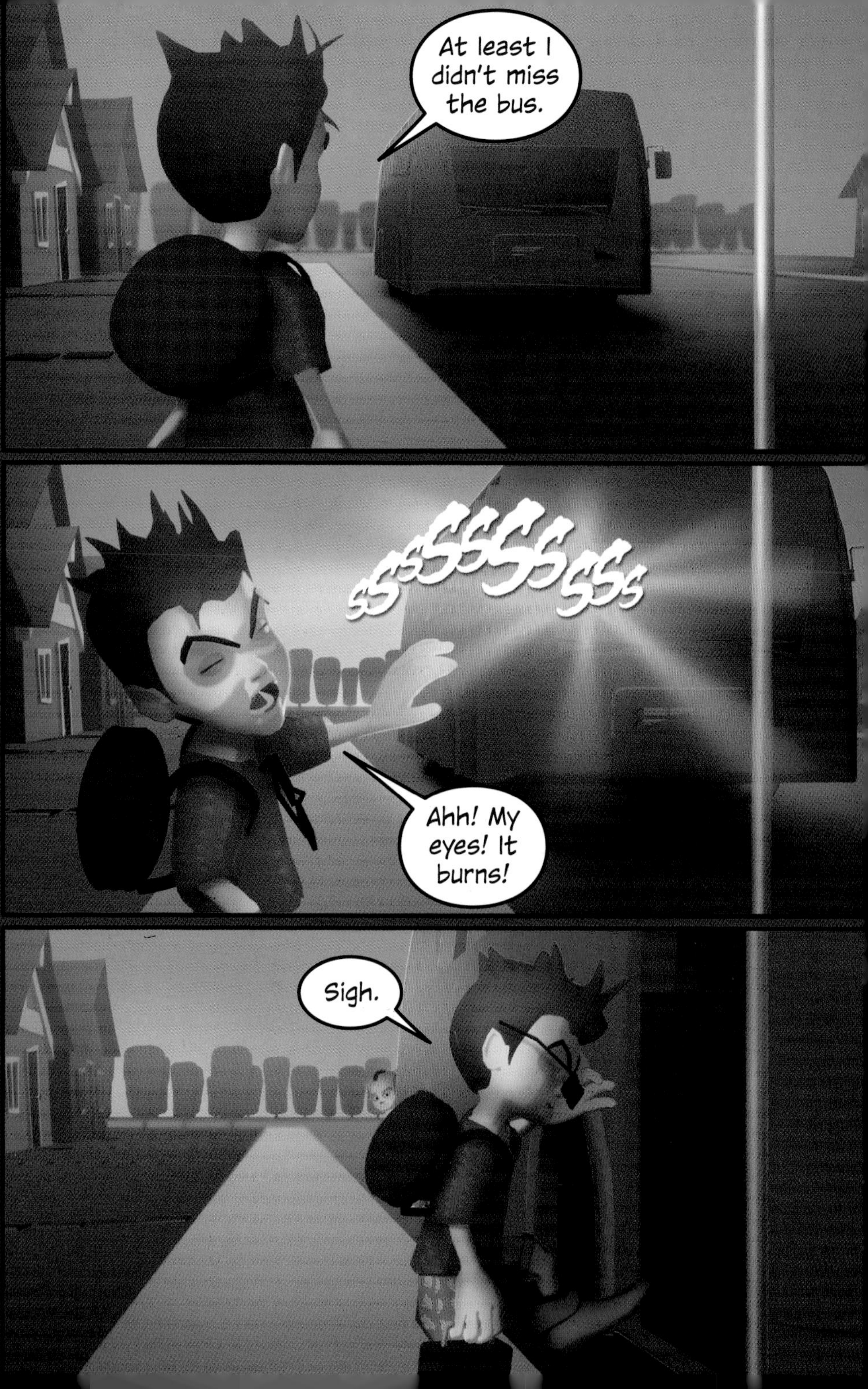
At least I didn't miss the bus.
sSsSSSSSSSSs
Ahh! My eyes! It burns!
Sigh.

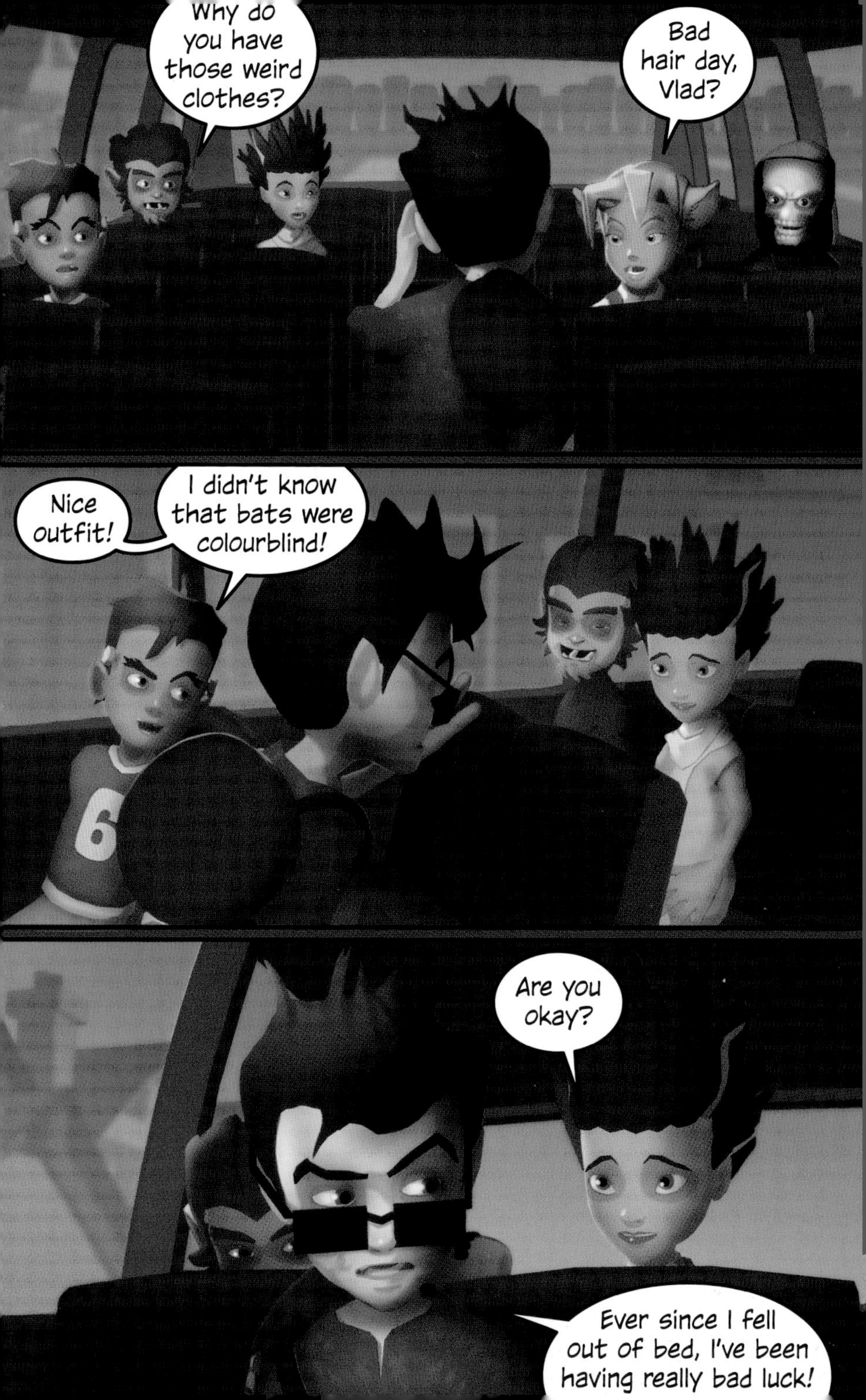
Why do you have those weird clothes?
Bad hair day, Vlad?
Nice outfit!
I didn't know that bats were colourblind!
Are you okay?
Ever since I fell out of bed, I've been having really bad luck!

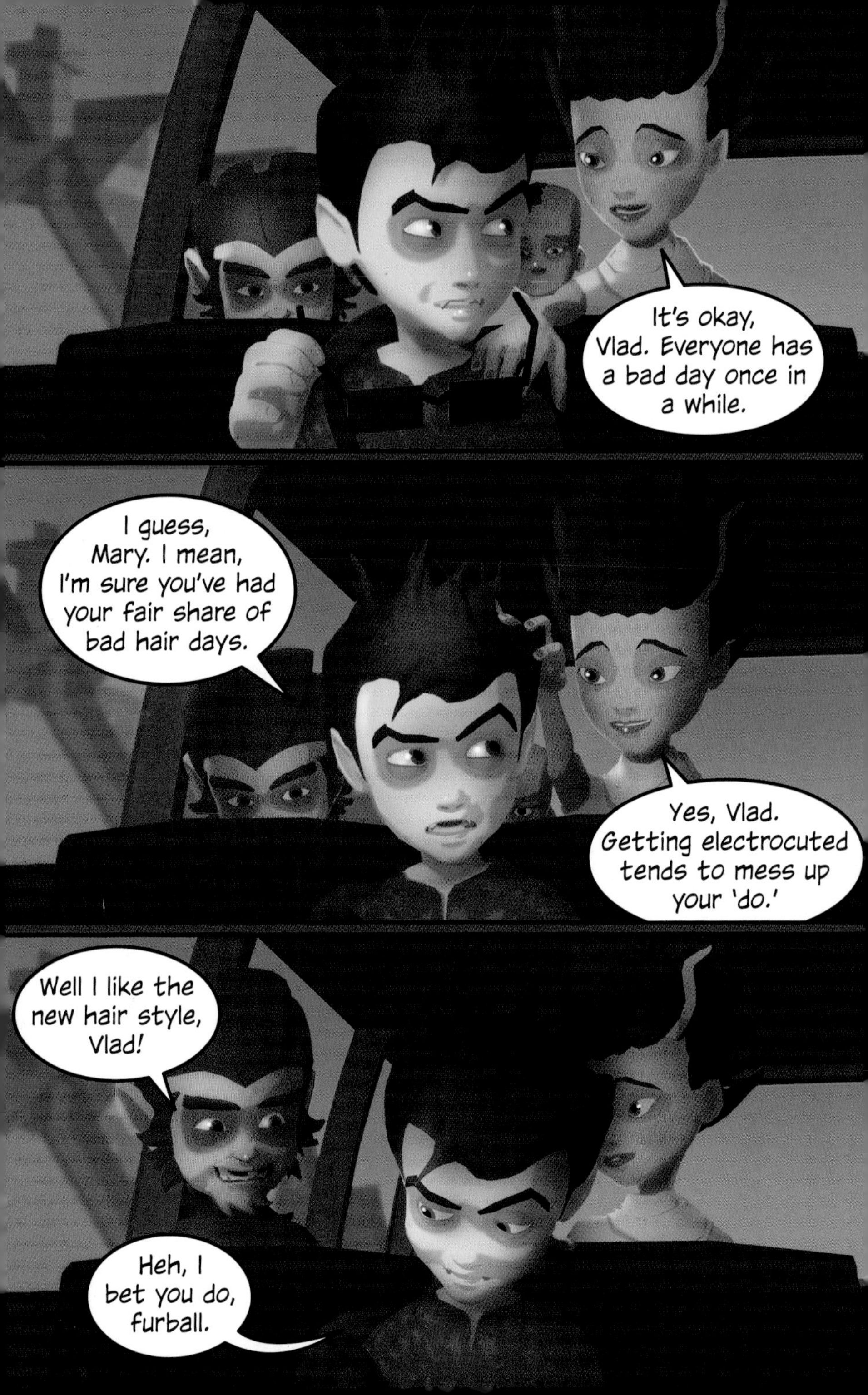
It's okay, Vlad. Everyone has a bad day once in a while.
I guess, Mary. I mean, I'm sure you've had your fair share of bad hair days.
Yes, Vlad. Getting electrocuted tends to mess up your 'do.'
Well I like the new hair style, Vlad!
Heh, I bet you do, furball.

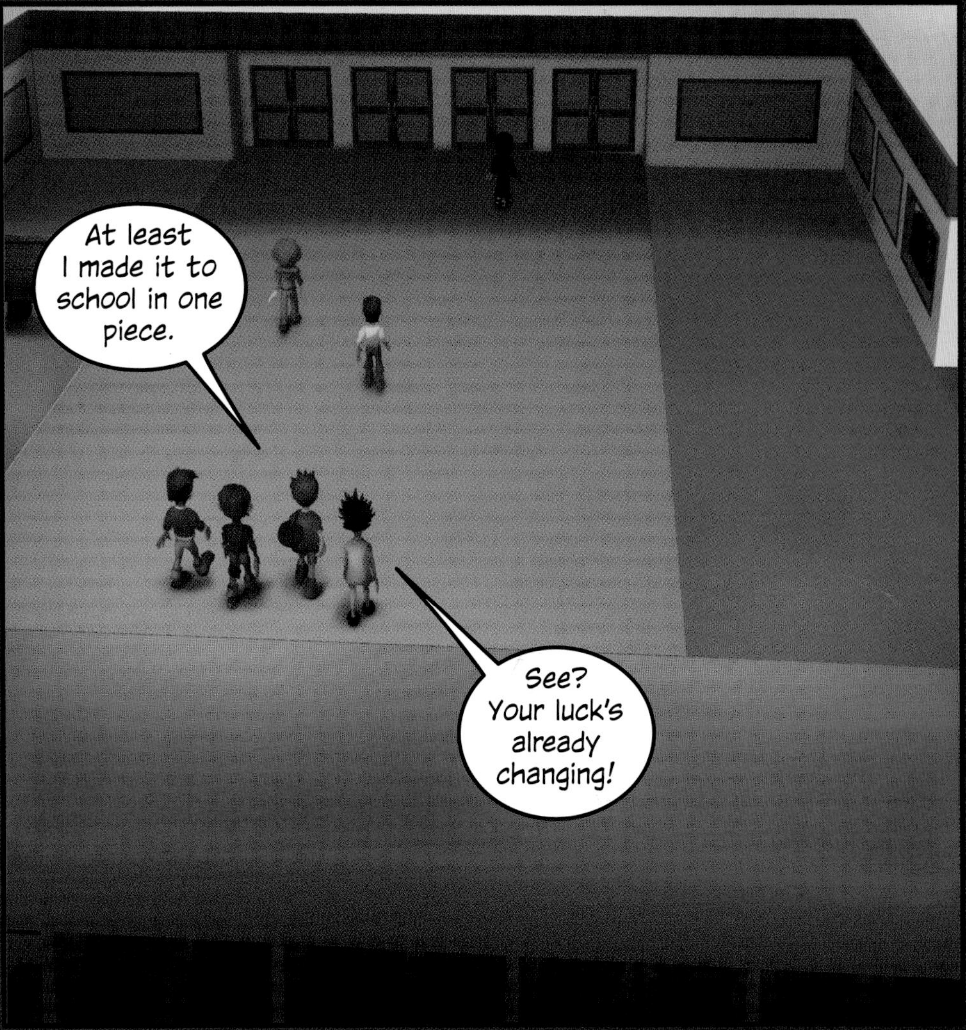
At least I made it to school in one piece.
See? Your luck's already changing!

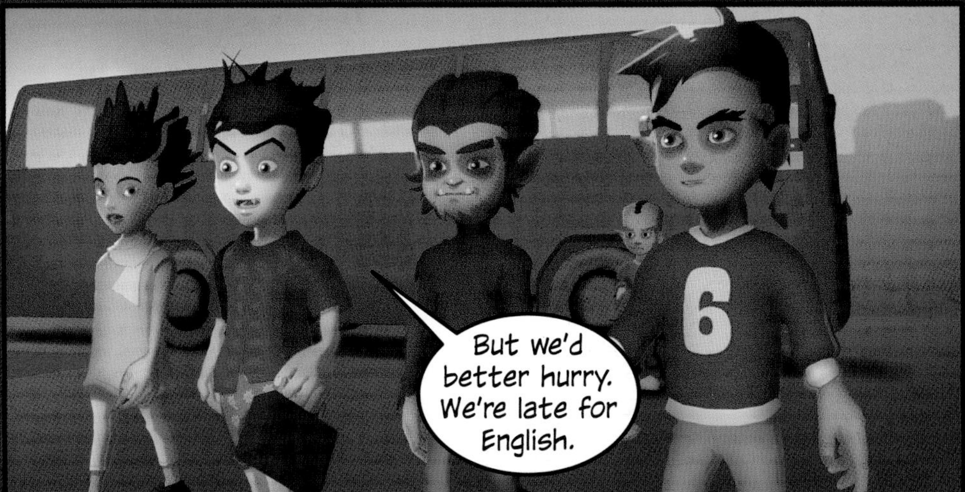
But we'd better hurry. We're late for English.

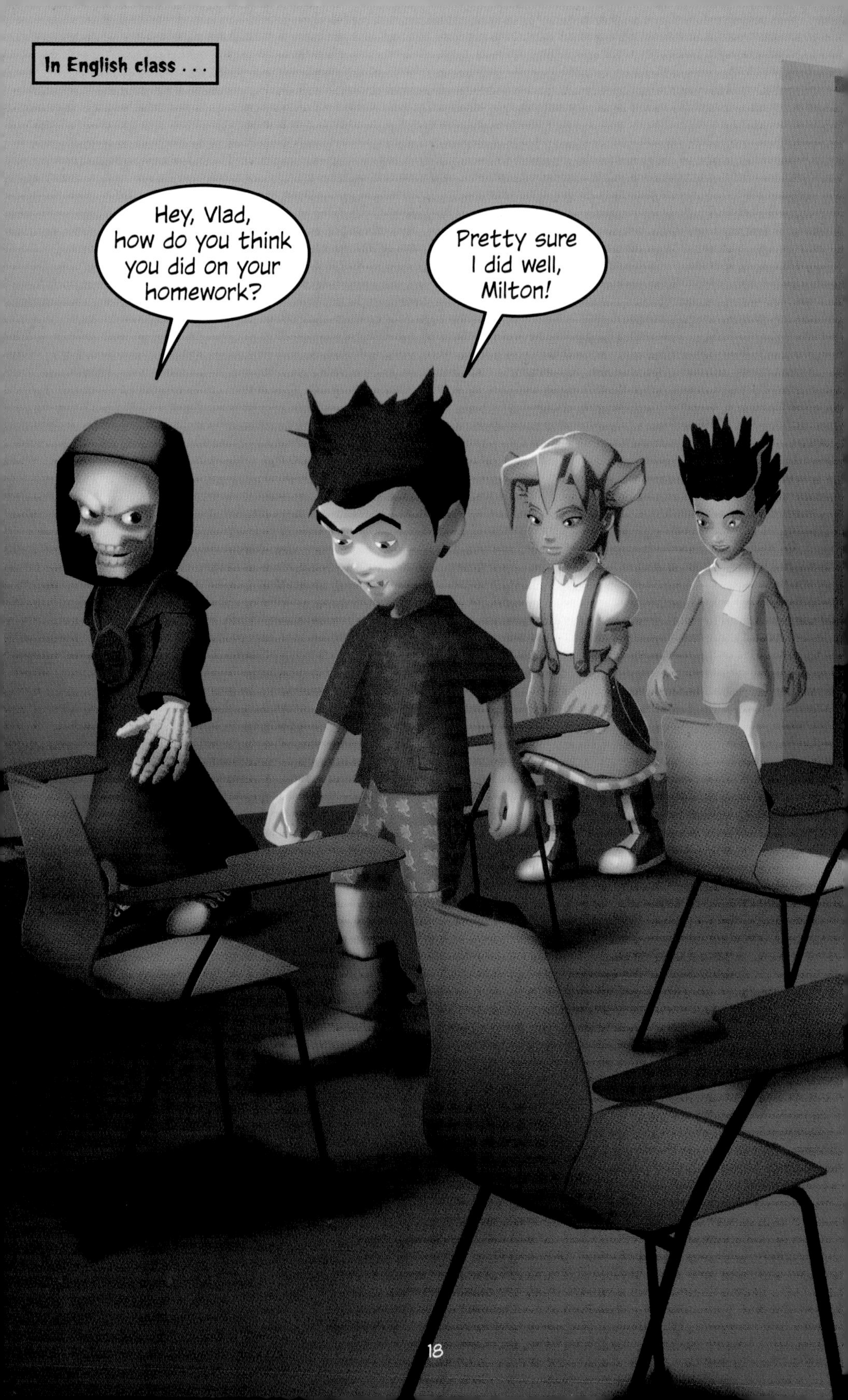
In English class . . .
Hey, Vlad, how do you think you did on your homework?
Pretty sure I did well, Milton!

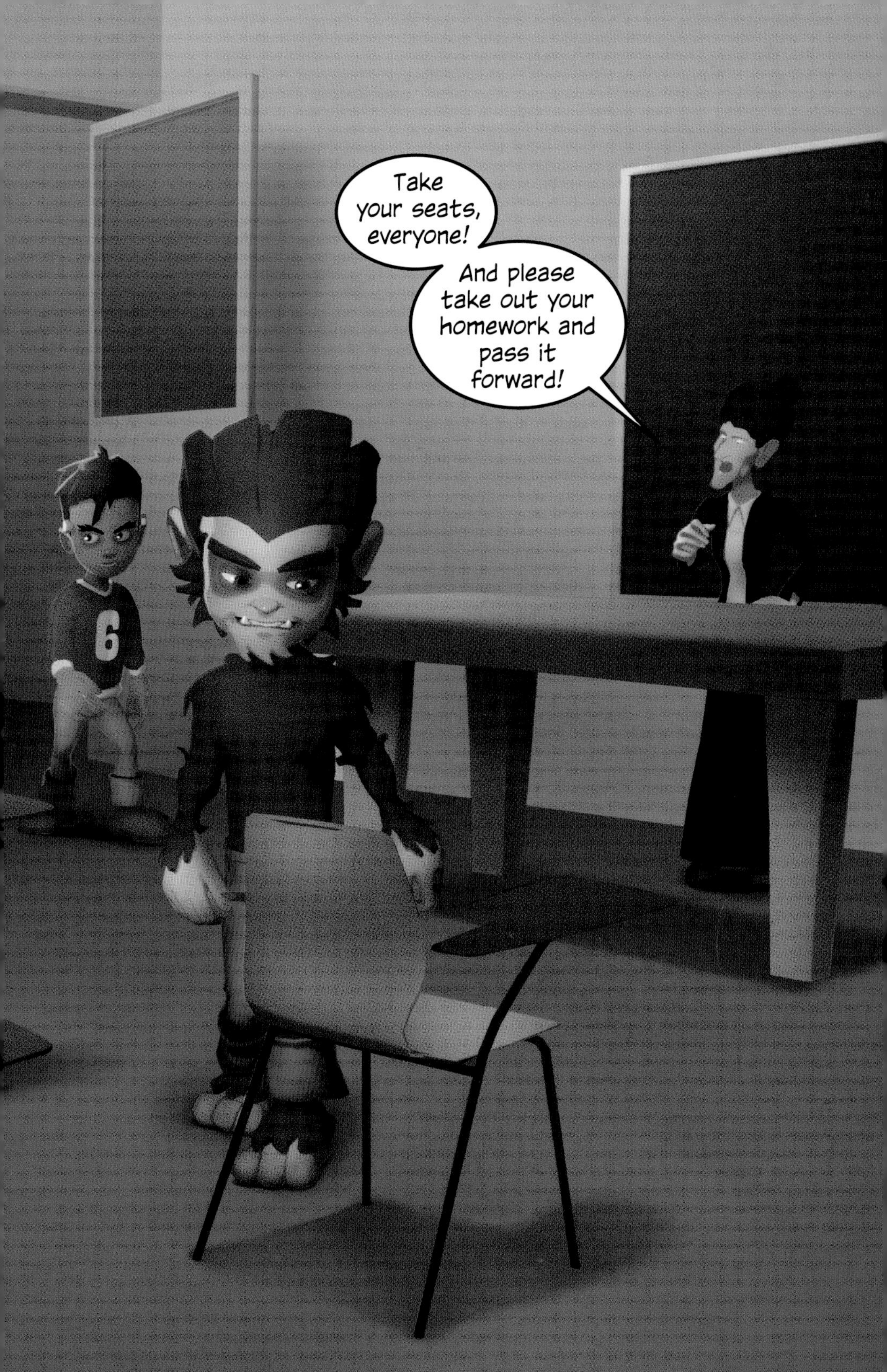
Take your seats, everyone!
And please take out your homework and pass it forward!

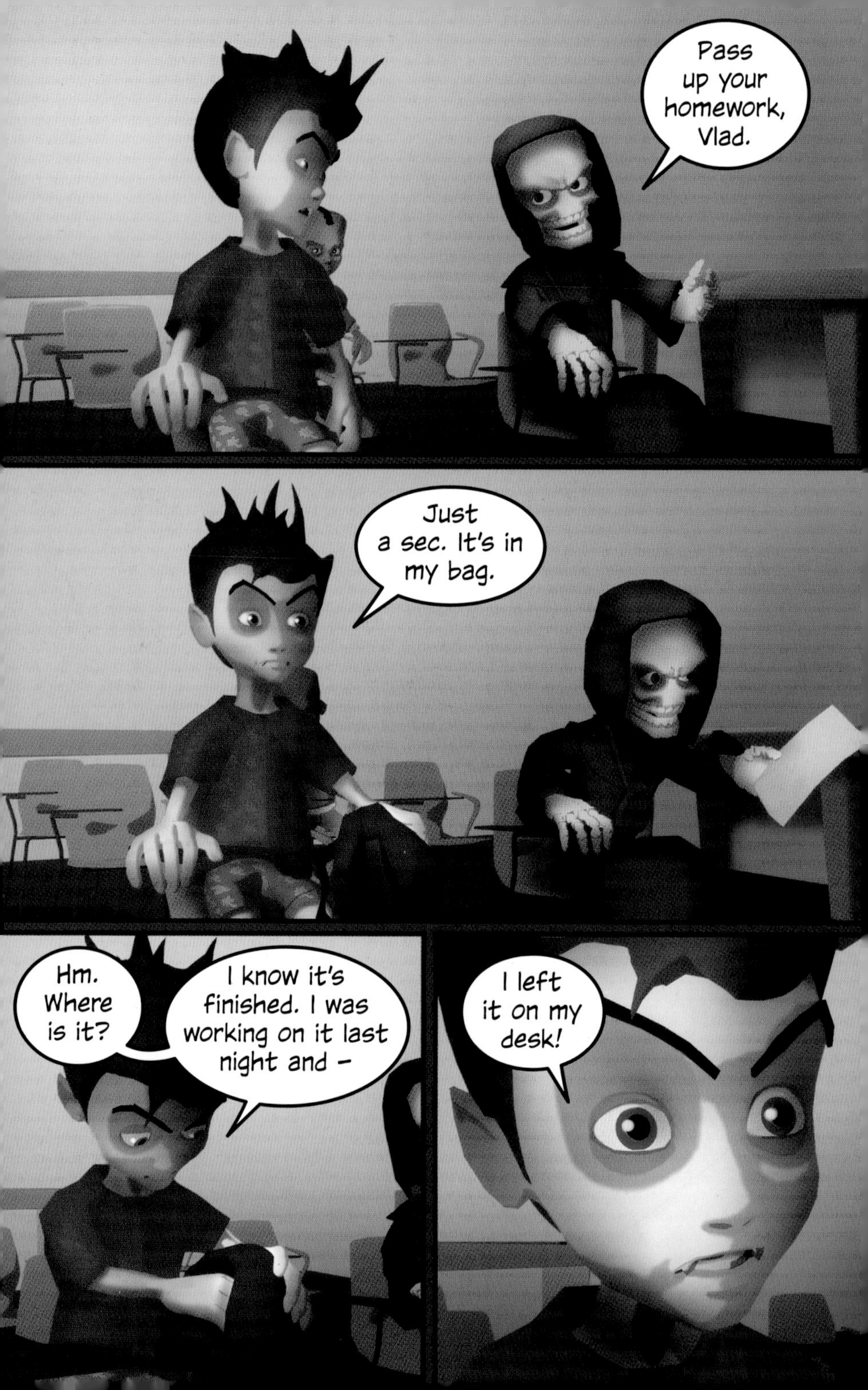
Pass up your homework, Vlad.
Just a sec. It's in my bag.
Hm. Where is it?
I know it's finished. I was working on it last night and –
I left it on my desk!

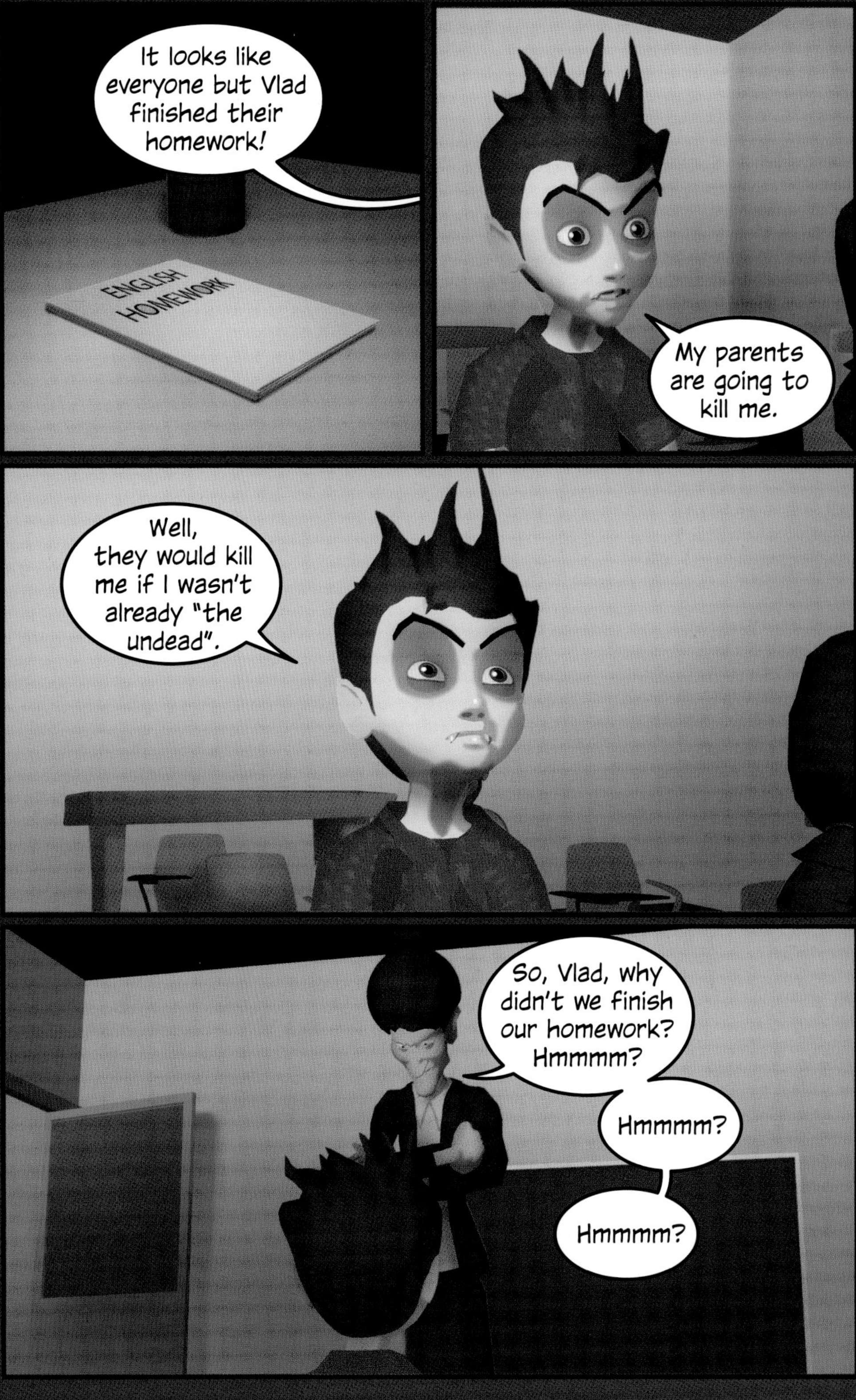
It looks like everyone but Vlad finished their homework!
ENGLISH HOMEWORK
My parents are going to kill me.
Well, they would kill me if I wasn't already "the undead".
So, Vlad, why didn't we finish our homework? Hmmmm?
Hmmmm?
Hmmmm?

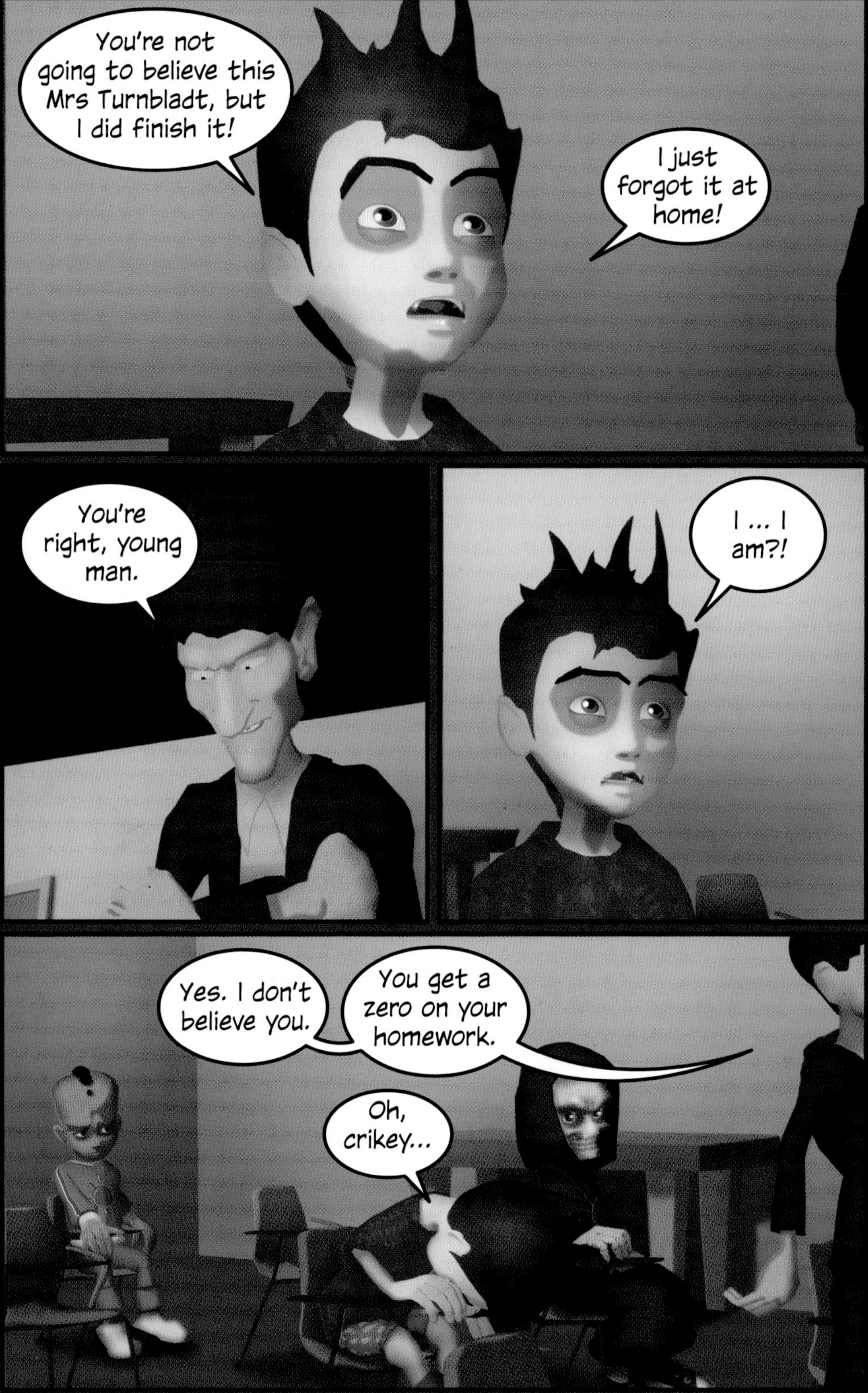
You're not going to believe this Mrs Turnbladt, but I did finish it!
I just forgot it at home!
You're right, young man.
I ... I am?!
Yes. I don't believe you.
You get a zero on your homework.
Oh, crikey...

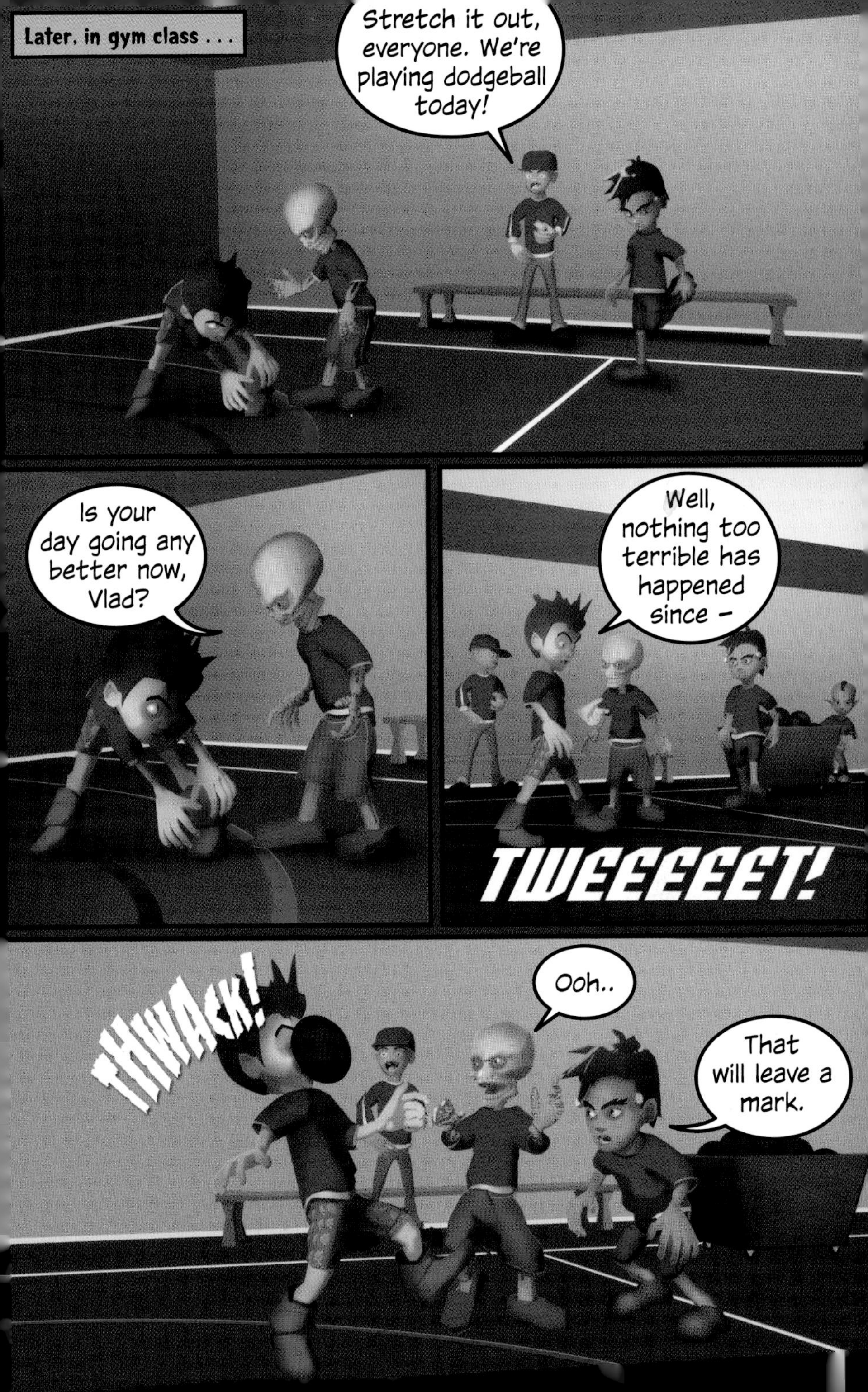
Later, in gym class . . .
Stretch it out, everyone. We're playing dodgeball today!
Is your day going any better now, Vlad?
Well, nothing too terrible has happened since –
TWEEEEET!
THWACK!
Ooh..
That will leave a mark.

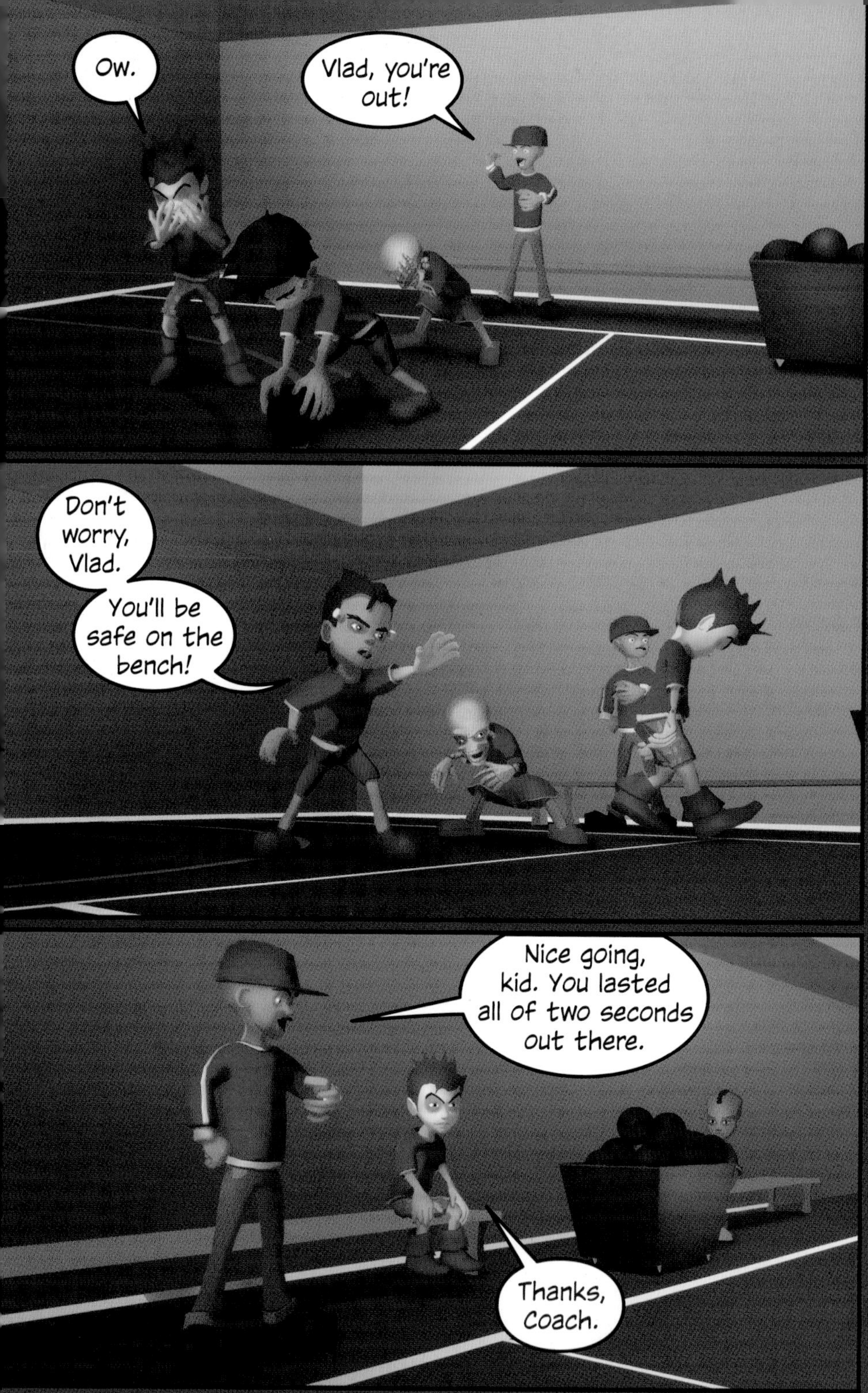
Ow.
Vlad, you're out!
Don't worry, Vlad.
You'll be safe on the bench!
Nice going, kid. You lasted all of two seconds out there.
Thanks, Coach.

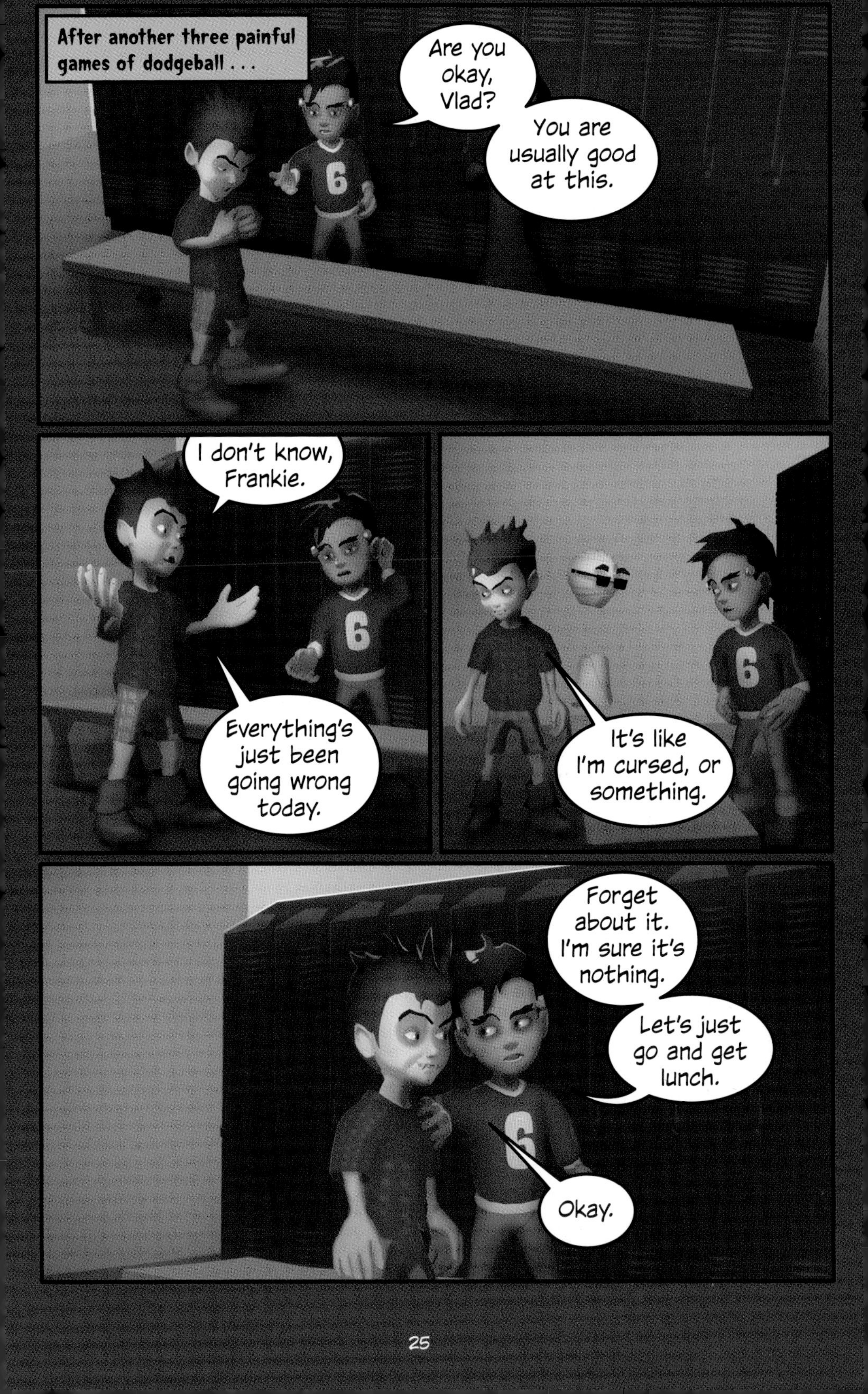
After another three painful games of dodgeball . . .
Are you okay, Vlad?
You are usually good at this.
I don't know, Frankie.
Everything's just been going wrong today.
It's like I'm cursed, or something.
Forget about it. I'm sure it's nothing.
Let's just go and get lunch.
Okay.

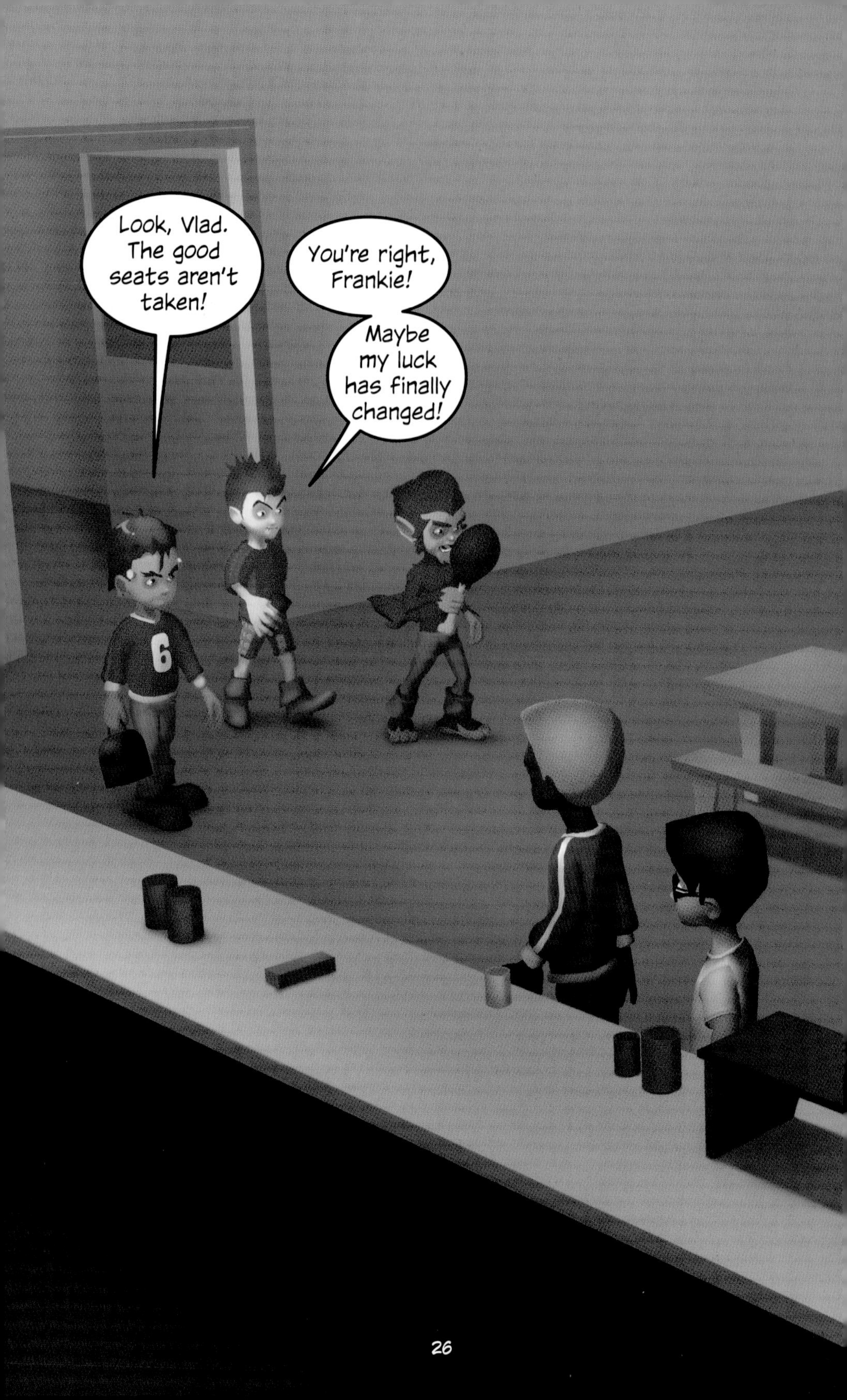
Look, Vlad. The good seats aren't taken!
You're right, Frankie!
Maybe my luck has finally changed!

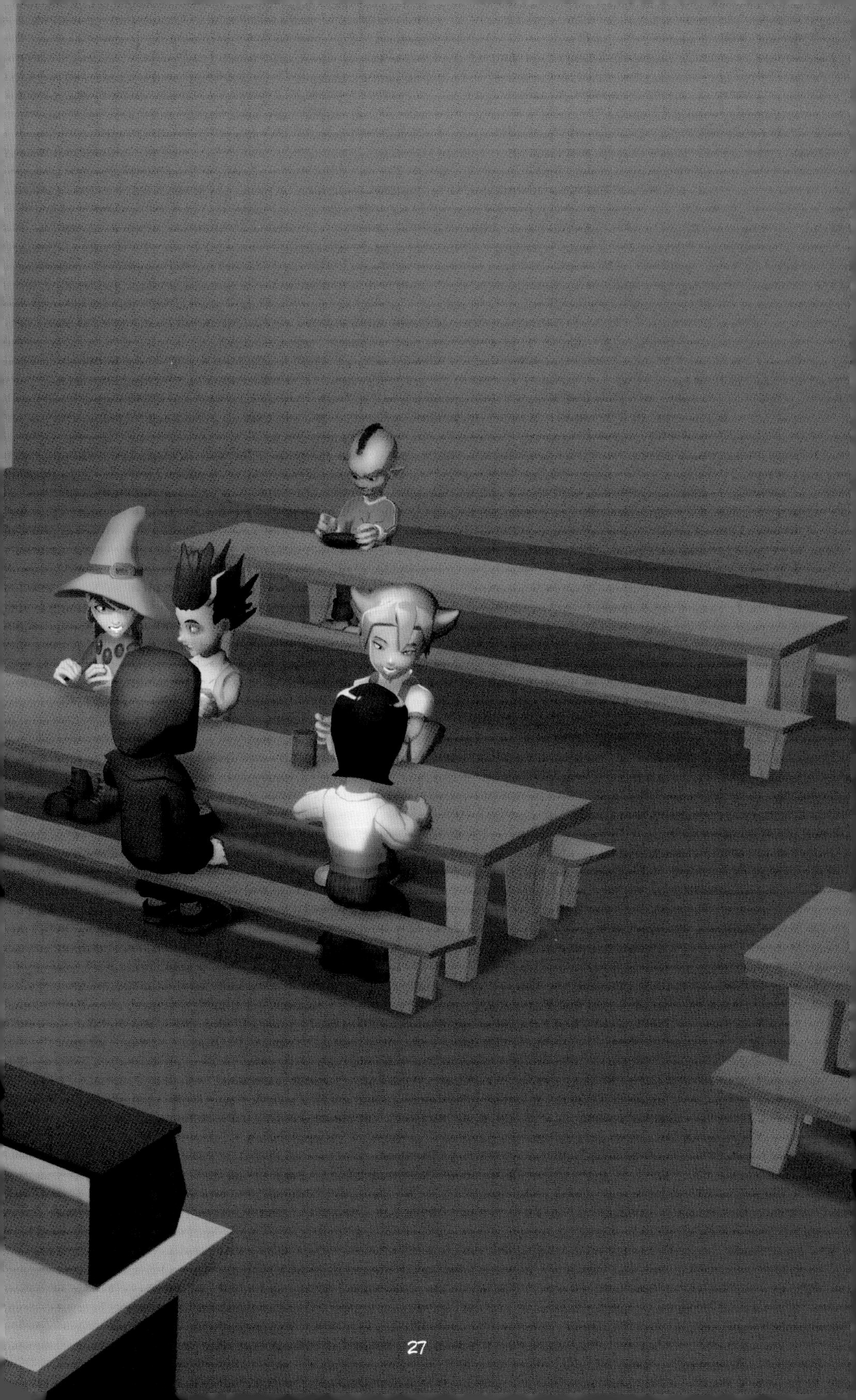

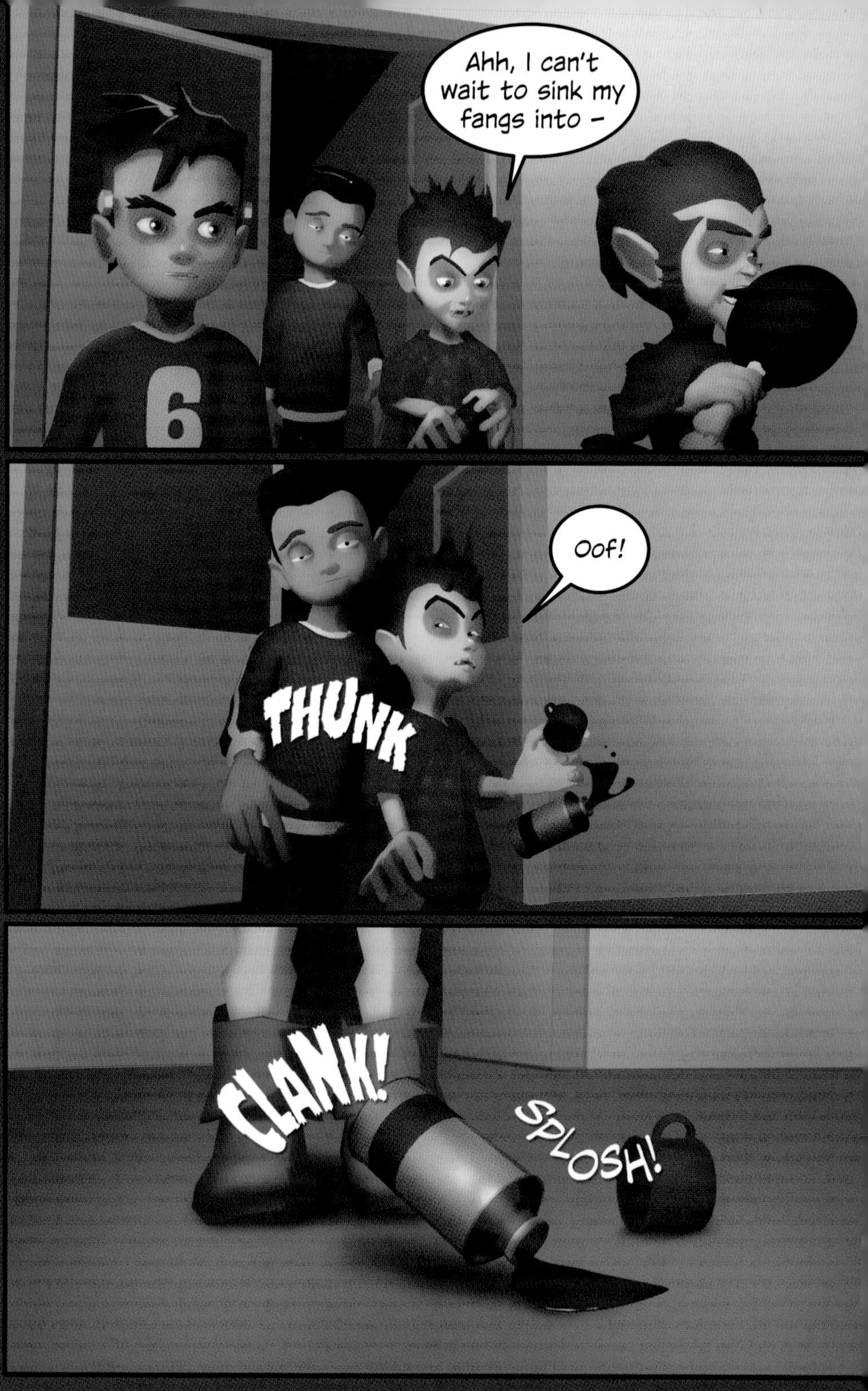
Ahh, I can't wait to sink my fangs into –
Oof!
THUNK
CLANK!
SPLOSH!

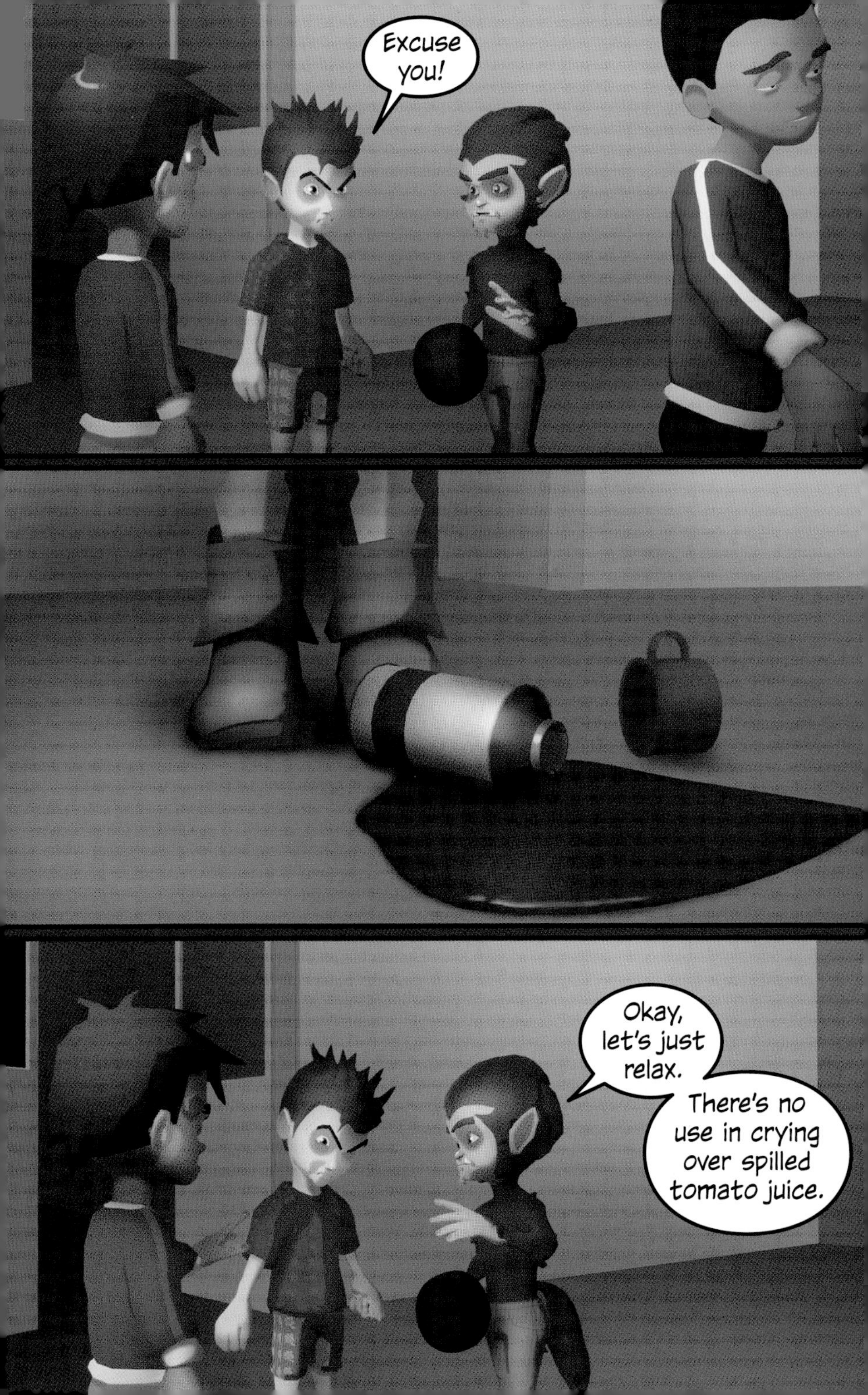
Excuse you!
Okay, let's just relax.
There's no use in crying over spilled tomato juice.

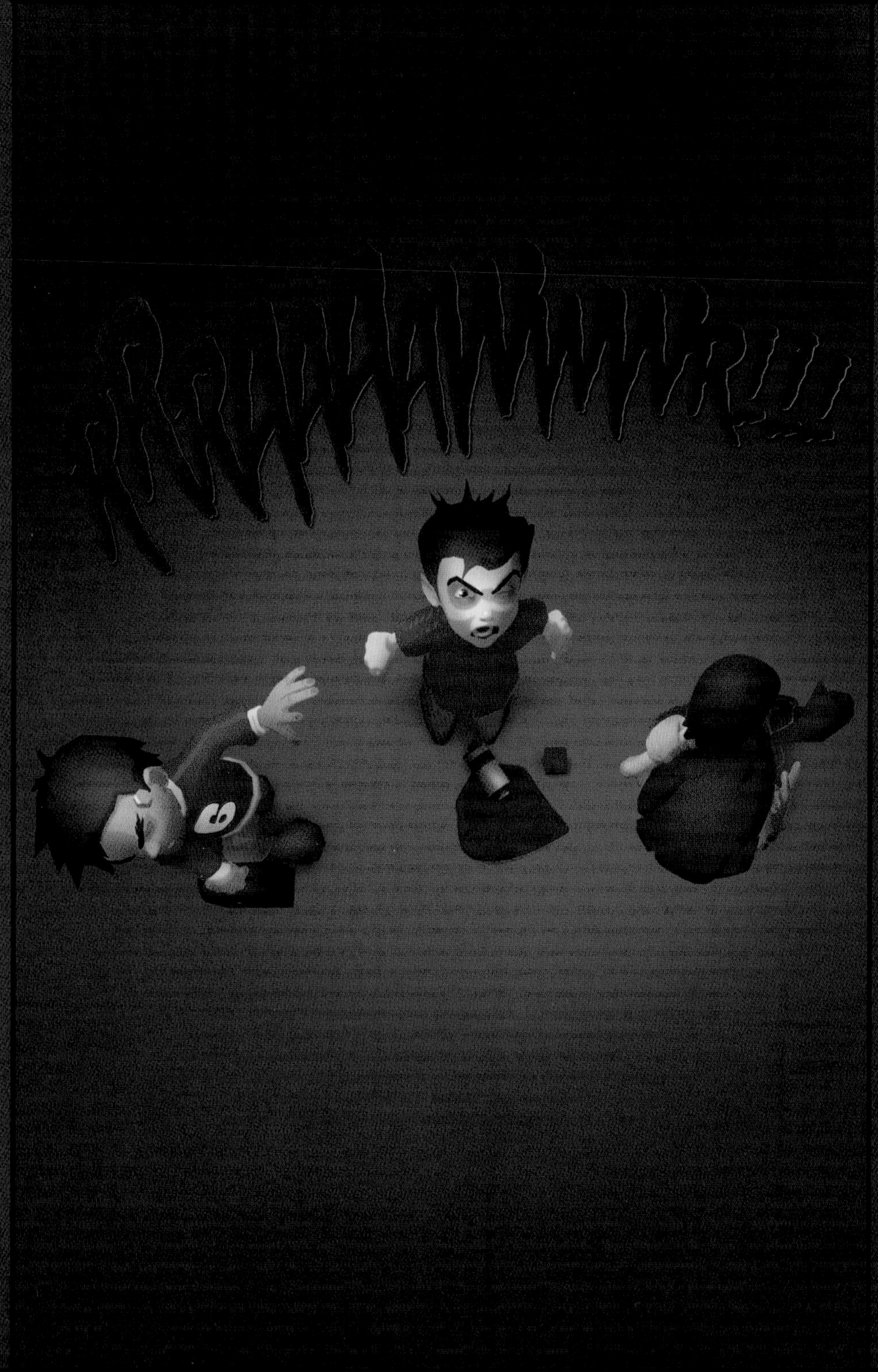

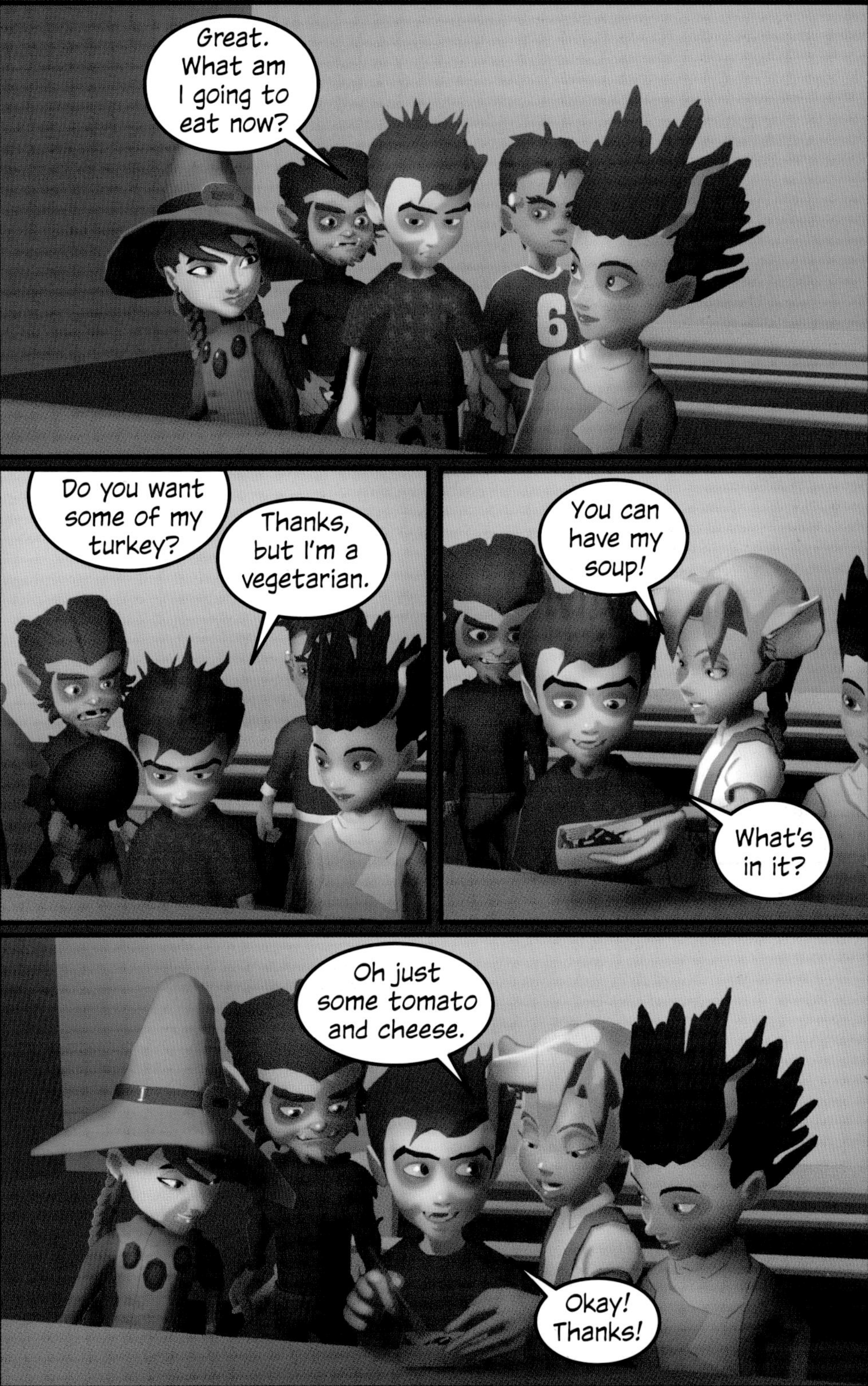
Great. What am I going to eat now?
Do you want some of my turkey?
Thanks, but I'm a vegetarian.
You can have my soup!
What's in it?
Oh just some tomato and cheese.
Okay! Thanks!

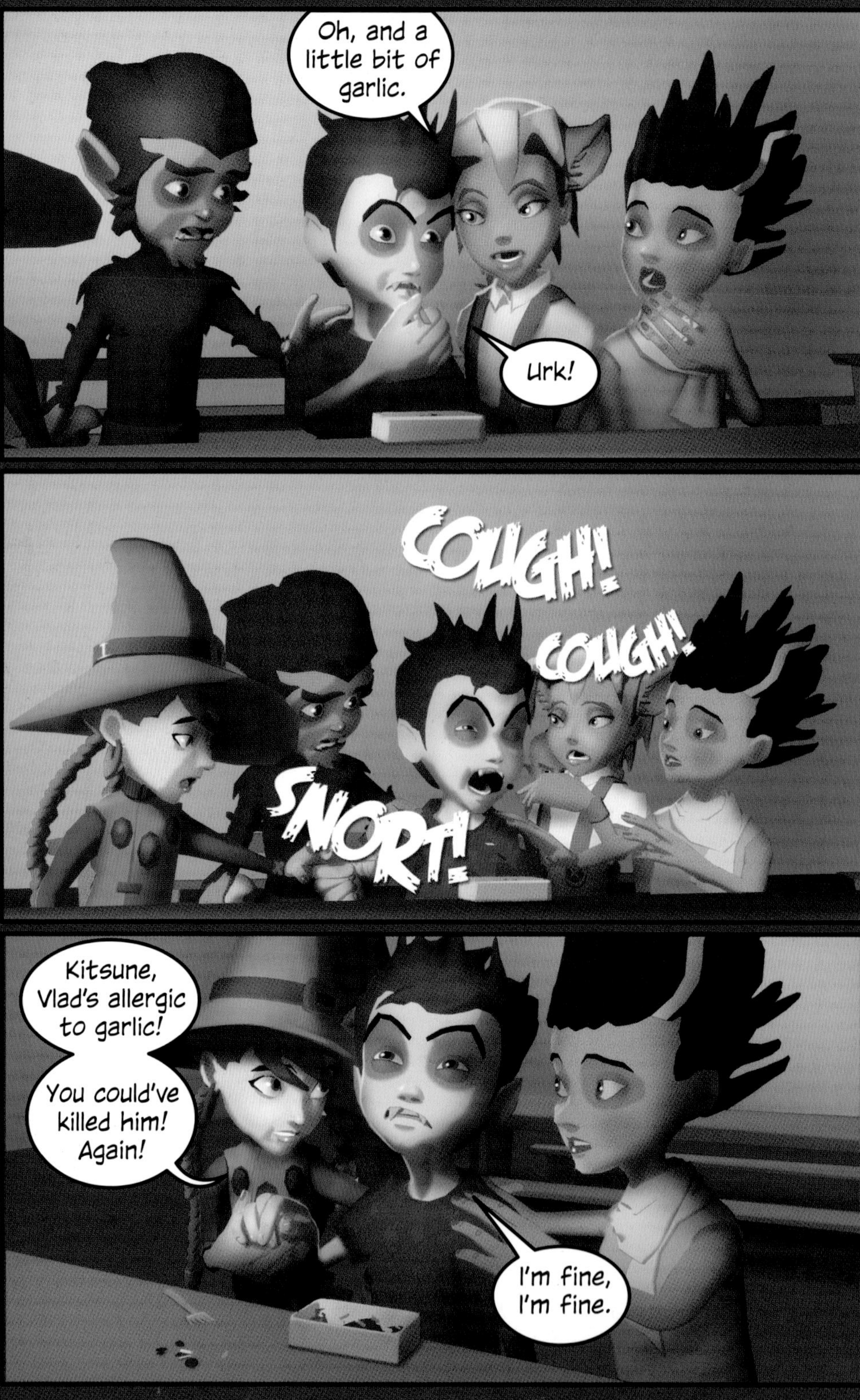
Oh, and a little bit of garlic.
Urk!
COUGH!
COUGH!
SNORT!
Kitsune, Vlad's allergic to garlic!
You could've killed him! Again!
I'm fine, I'm fine.

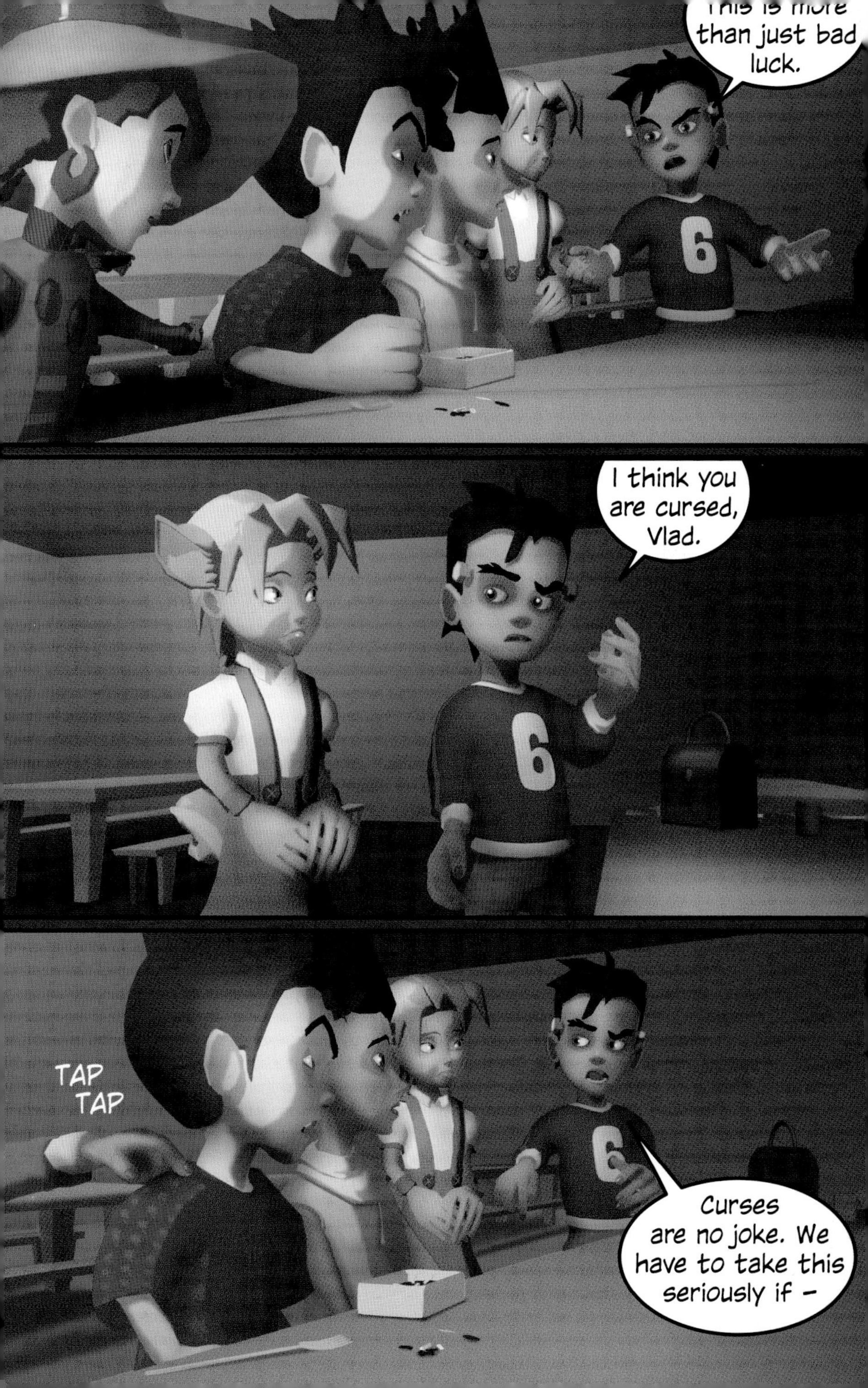
than just bad luck.
I think you are cursed, Vlad.
TAP TAP
Curses are no joke. We have to take this seriously if –

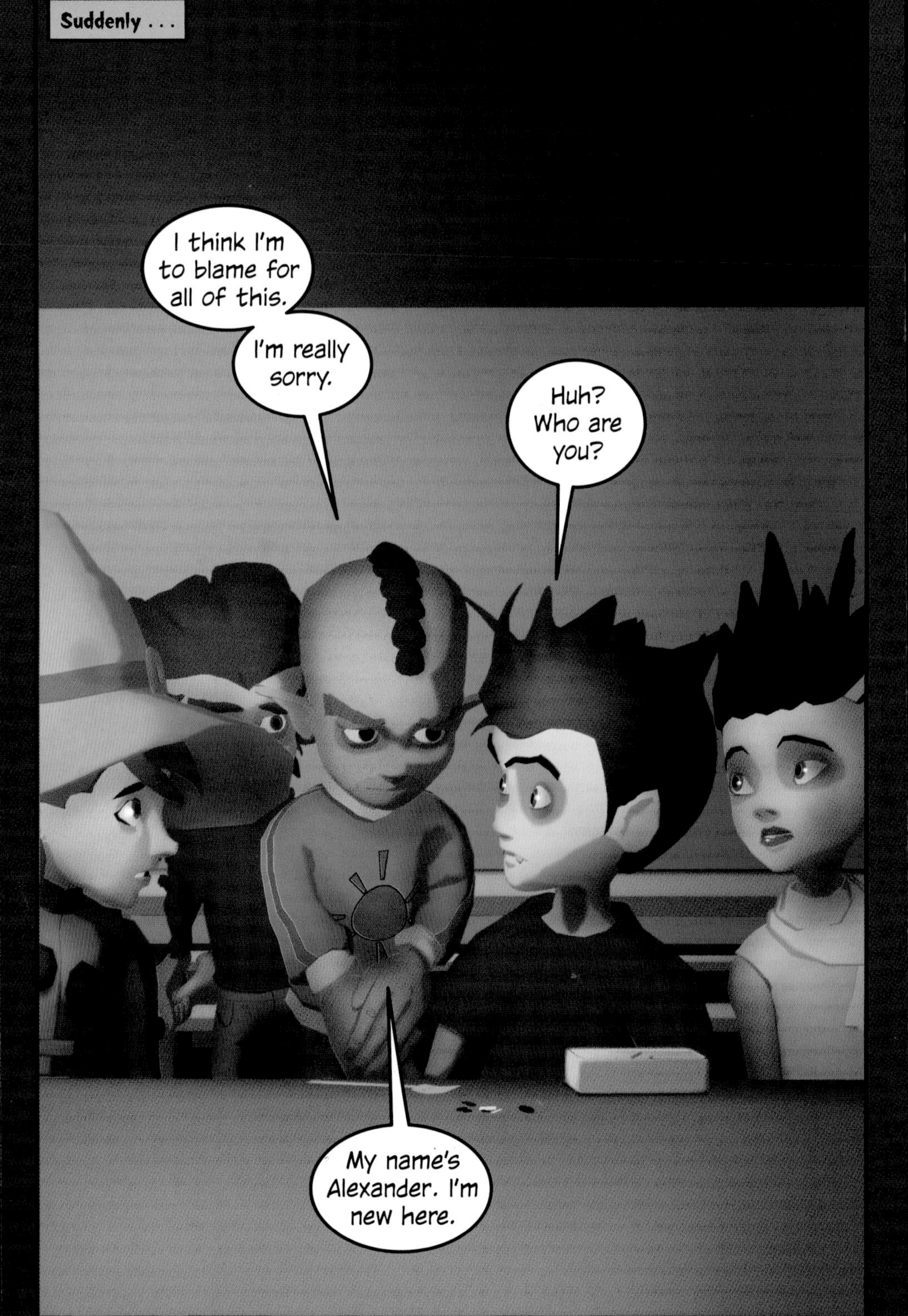
Suddenly . . .
I think I'm to blame for all of this.
I'm really sorry.
Huh? Who are you?
My name's Alexander. I'm new here.

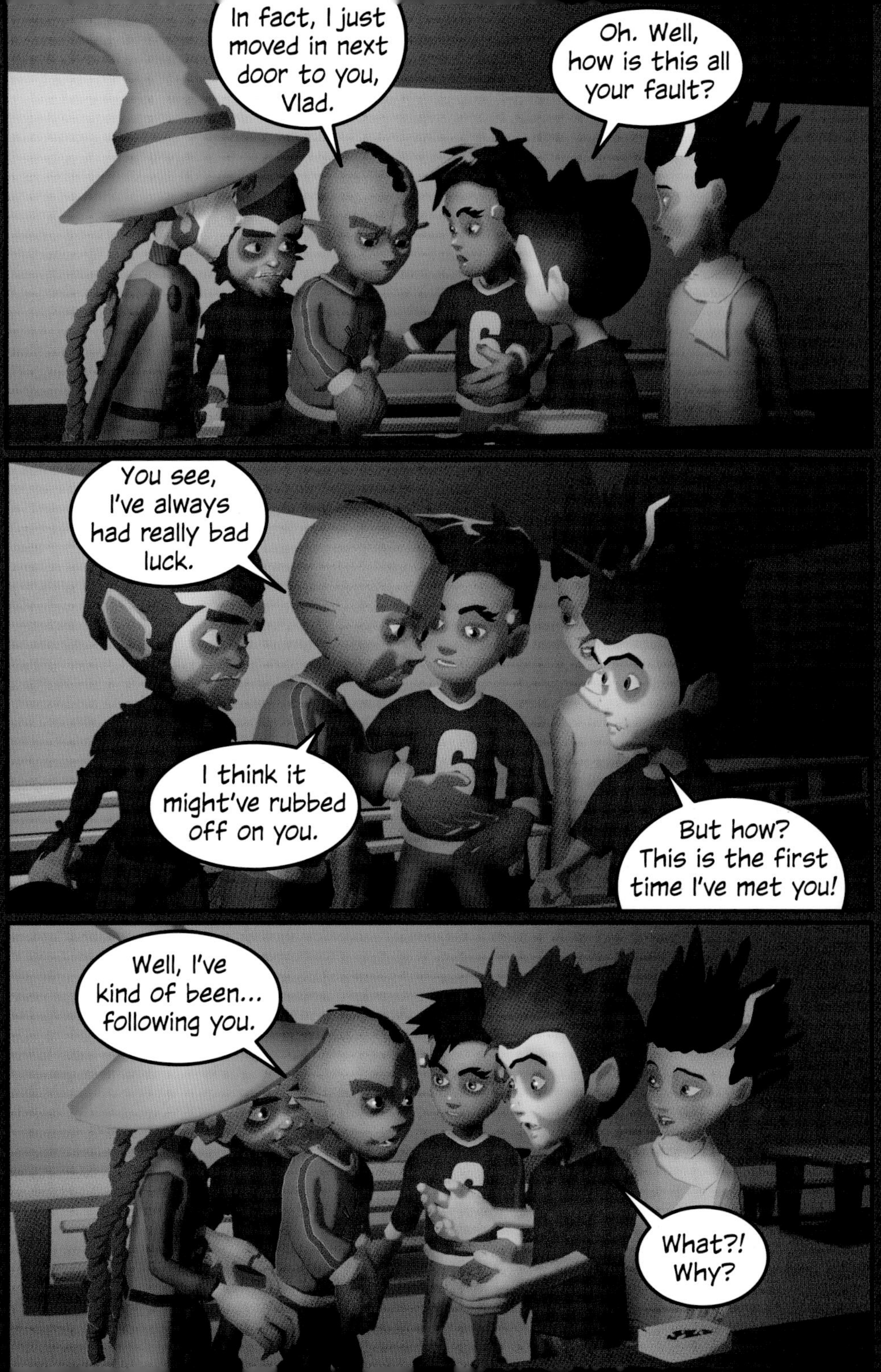
In fact, I just moved in next door to you, Vlad.
Oh. Well, how is this all your fault?
You see, I've always had really bad luck.
I think it might've rubbed off on you.
But how? This is the first time I've met you!
Well, I've kind of been... following you.
What?! Why?

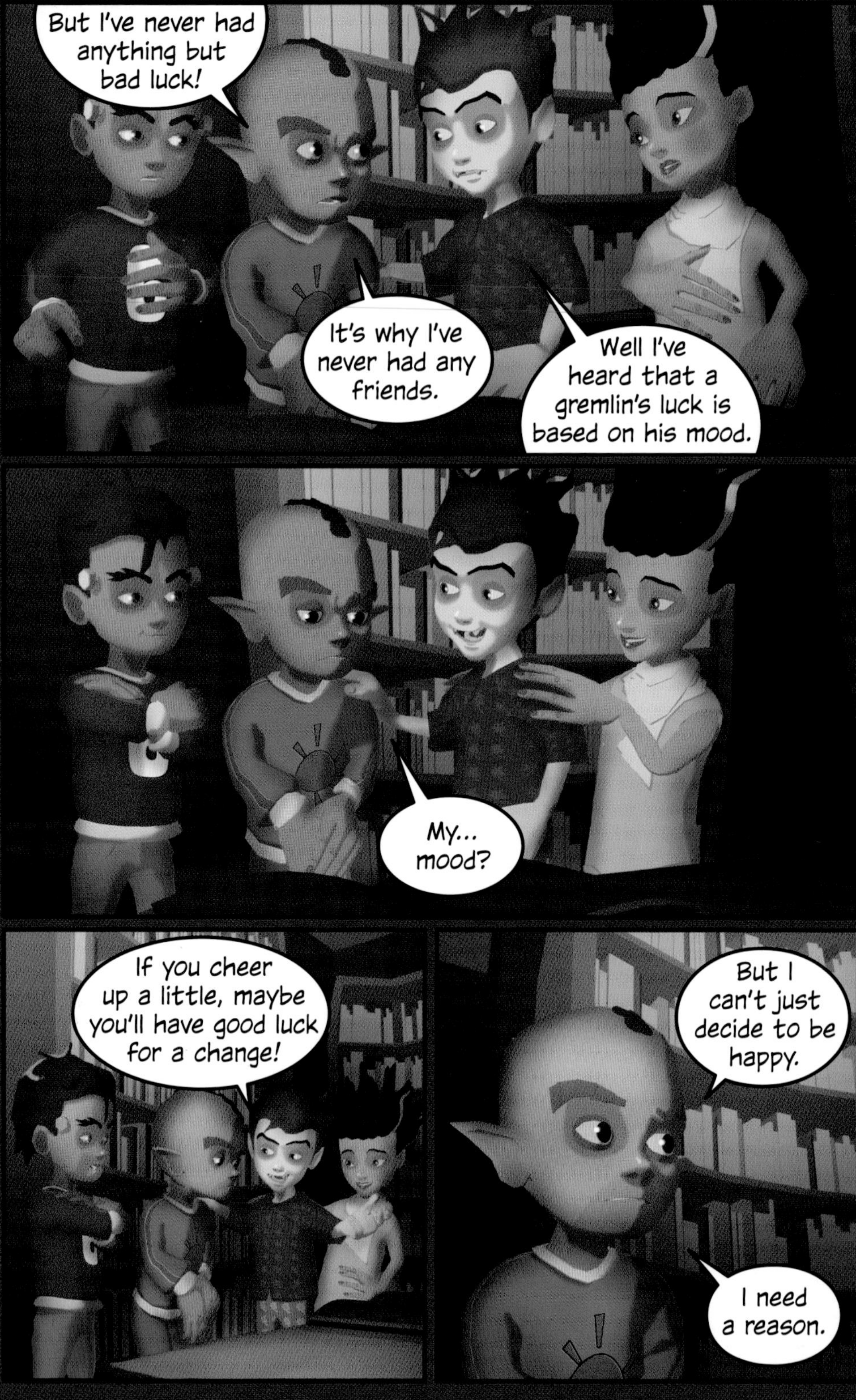

But I've never had anything but bad luck!
It's why I've never had any friends.
Well I've heard that a gremlin's luck is based on his mood.
My... mood?
If you cheer up a little, maybe you'll have good luck for a change!
But I can't just decide to be happy.
I need a reason.

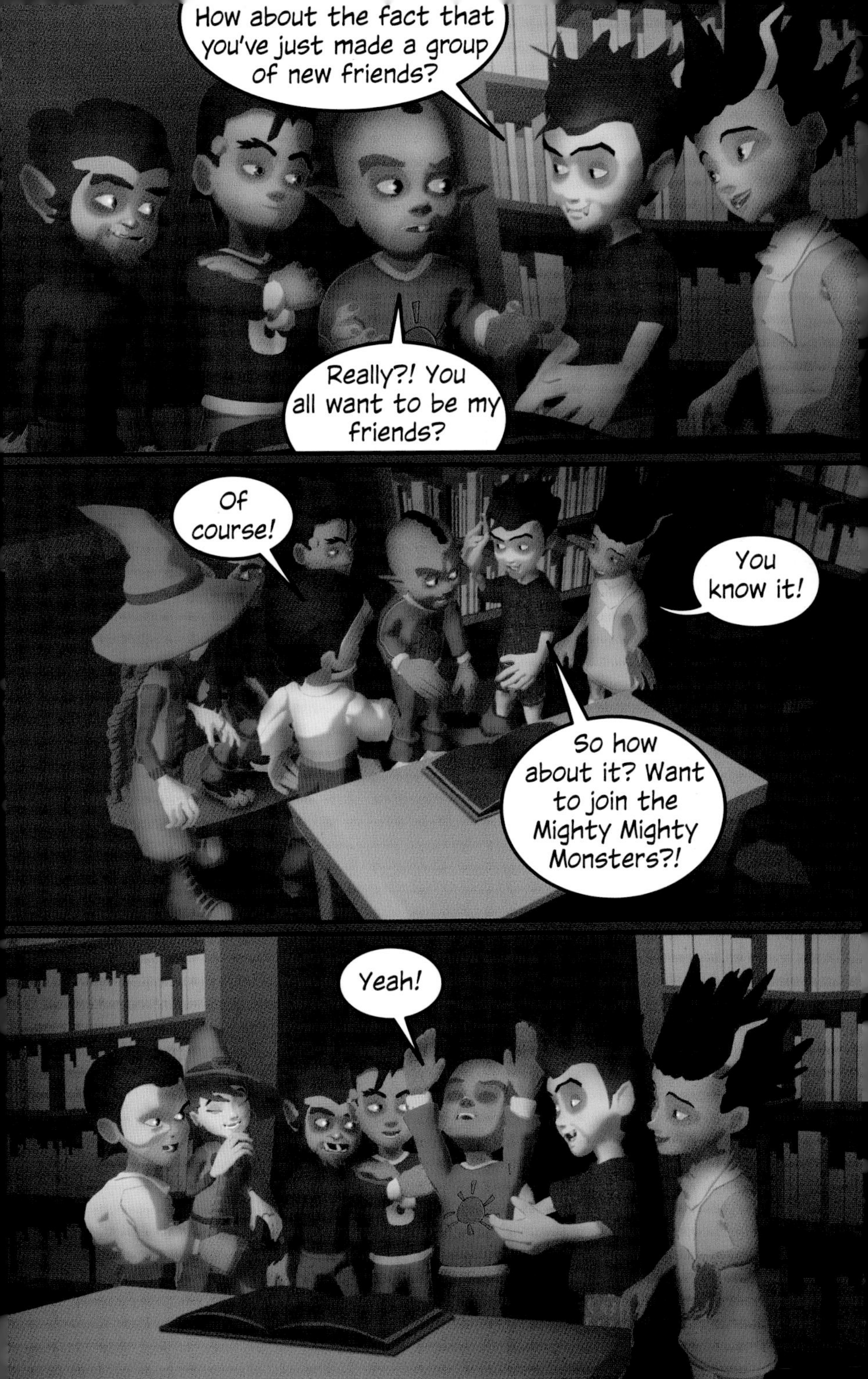
How about the fact that you've just made a group of new friends?
Really?! You all want to be my friends?
Of course!
You know it!
So how about it? Want to join the Mighty Mighty Monsters?!
Yeah!

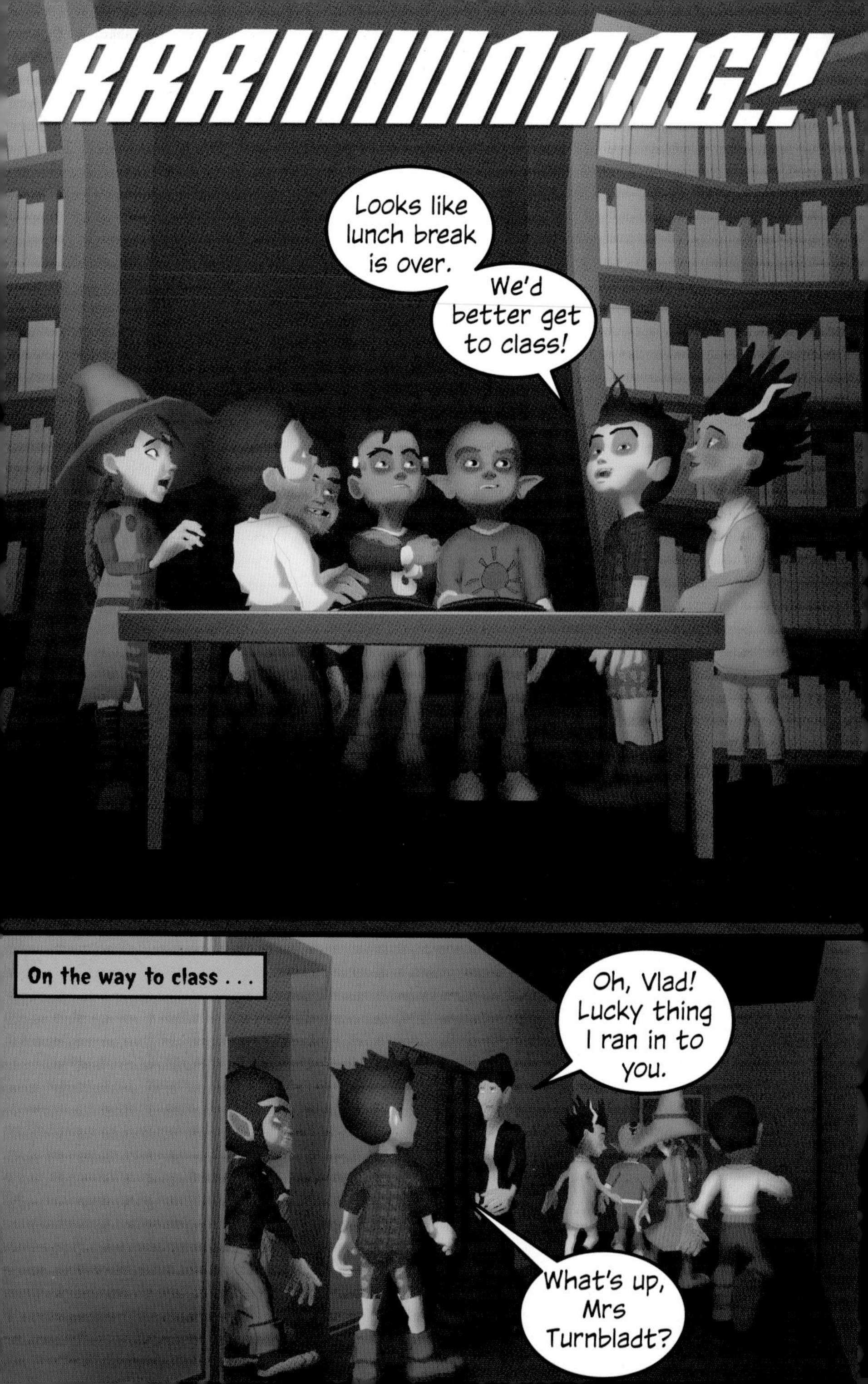
RRRIIIIINNNG!!
Looks like lunch break is over.
We'd better get to class!
On the way to class . . .
Oh, Vlad! Lucky thing I ran in to you.
What's up, Mrs Turnbladt?

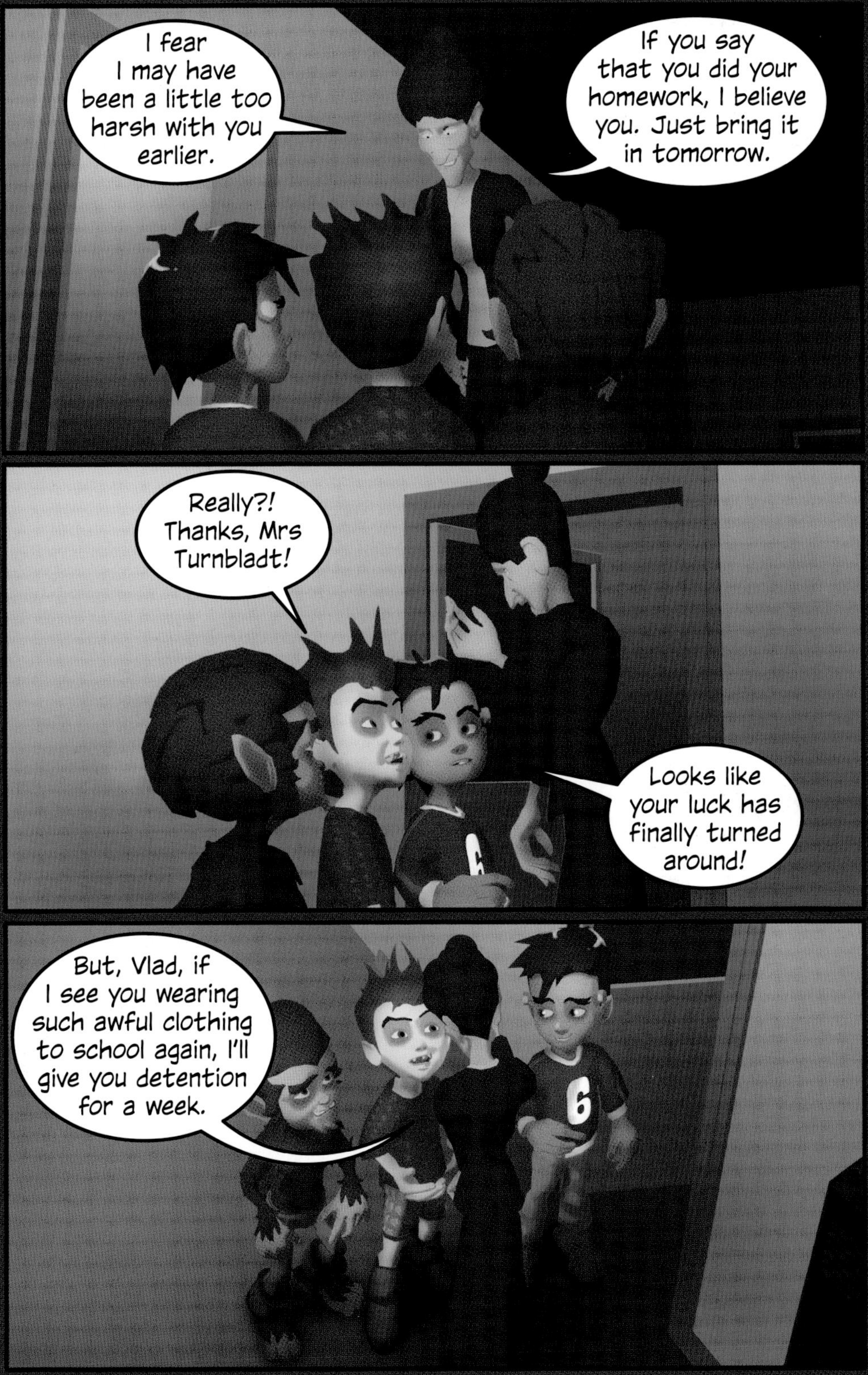
I fear I may have been a little too harsh with you earlier.
If you say that you did your homework, I believe you. Just bring it in tomorrow.
Really?! Thanks, Mrs Turnbladt!
Looks like your luck has finally turned around!
But, Vlad, if I see you wearing such awful clothing to school again, I'll give you detention for a week.

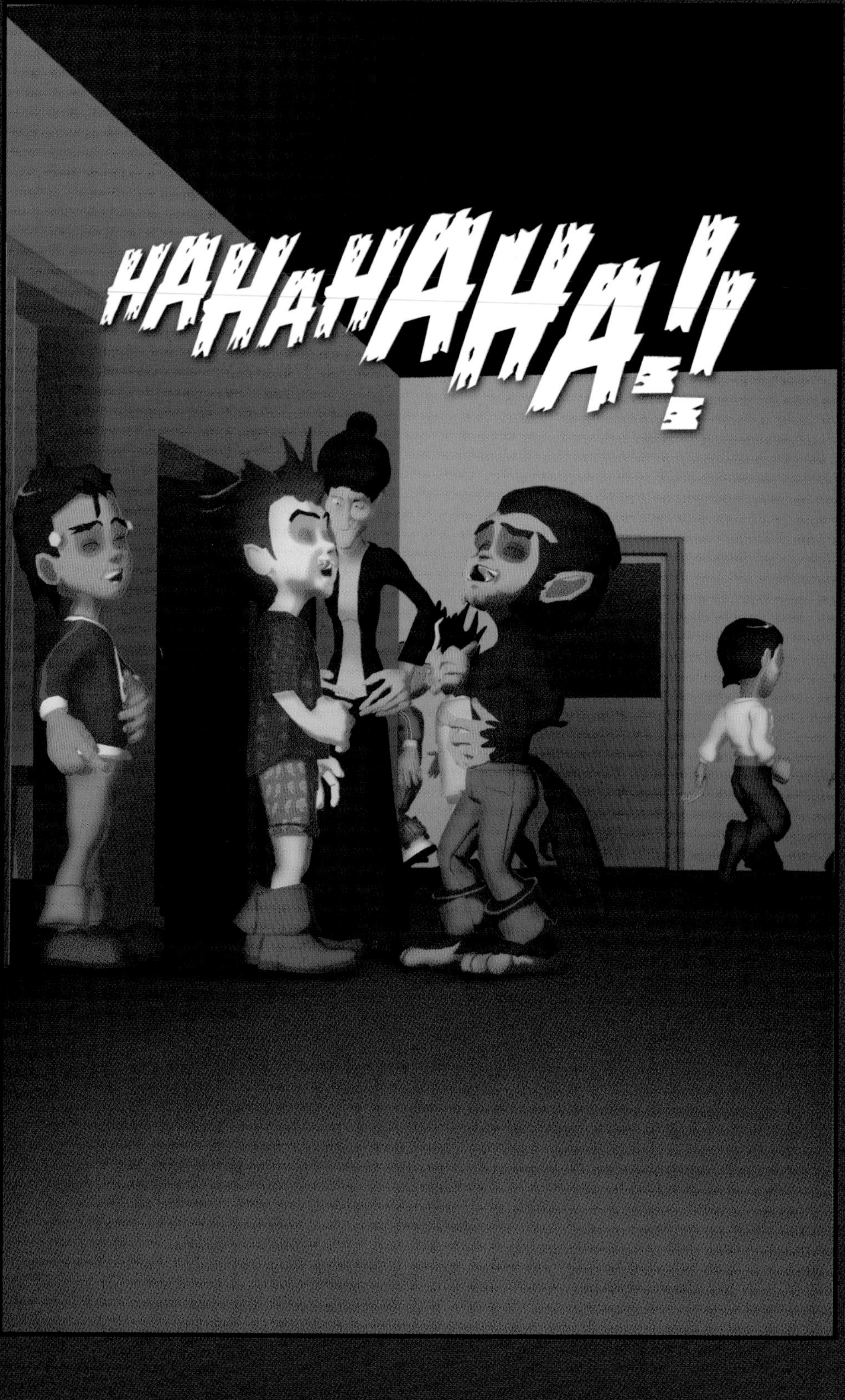
HAHAHAHAHA!

ABOUT
SEAN O'REILLY
AND ARCANA STUDIO

As a lifelong comics fan, Sean O'Reilly dreamed of becoming a comic book creator. In 2004, he realized that dream by creating Arcana Studio. In one short year, O'Reilly took his studio from a one-person operation in his basement to an award-winning comic book publisher with more than 150 graphic novels produced for Harper Collins, Simon & Schuster, Random House, Scholastic and others.

Within a year, the company won many awards including the Shuster Award for Outstanding Publisher and the Moonbeam Award for top children's graphic novel. O'Reilly also won the Top 40 Under 40 award from the city of Vancouver and authored *The Clockwork Girl* for Top Graphic Novel at Book Expo America in 2009. Currently, O'Reilly is one of the most prolific independent comic book writers in Canada. While showing no signs of slowing down in comics, he now writes screenplays and adapts his creations for the big screen.

GLOSSARY

breed (BREED)—a particular type of animal

colourblind (KUHL-uh-blined) – if you are colourblind, you cannot see certain colours

curse (KURSS) – an evil spell

electrocuted (i-LEK-truh-kyoo-tid) – injured or killed by a severe electric shock

gremlin (GREM-lin) – a mischievous being that can cause trouble for others

knack (NAK) – an ability to do something difficult or tricky

relax (ri-LAKS) – become less tense and anxious

typical (TIP-i-kuhl) – normal, or in a usual way

undead (un-DED) – no longer alive, but instead animated by a supernatural force, for example, a vampire or zombie

vegetarian (vej-uh-TARE-ee-uhn)—someone who eats only plants

DISCUSSION QUESTIONS

1. Do you believe in good luck? How about bad luck? Why or why not?

2. Poto brings the other monsters to the library to find information about gremlins. When you go to the library, what do you look for? What are your favourite books? Talk about it.

3. Alexander struggles to find friends as the new boy in school. Have you ever been new at a school? What do you think it's like to not know anyone at your school? Talk about the challenges in what happened.

WRITING PROMPTS

1. Alexander the gremlin has trouble making friends. How many friends do you have? Do you wish you had more friends? Write about friendship.

2. Vlad has a bad hair day and has to wear mismatched clothing to school. What are some other embarrassing things that could happen to someone at school? Write about a pupil's really bad school day.

3. Mrs Turnbladt punishes Vlad for forgetting to bring his homework to school. Have you ever been punished for something in school? What happened? Write about it.

Mighty
Mighty
MONSTERS
ADVENTURES

The KING of HALLOWEEN CASTLE

HIDE and SHRIEK!

Lost in SPOOKY FOREST

My MISSING MONSTER

NEW MONSTER in SCHOOL

MONSTER MANSION

THE MONSTER CROOKS

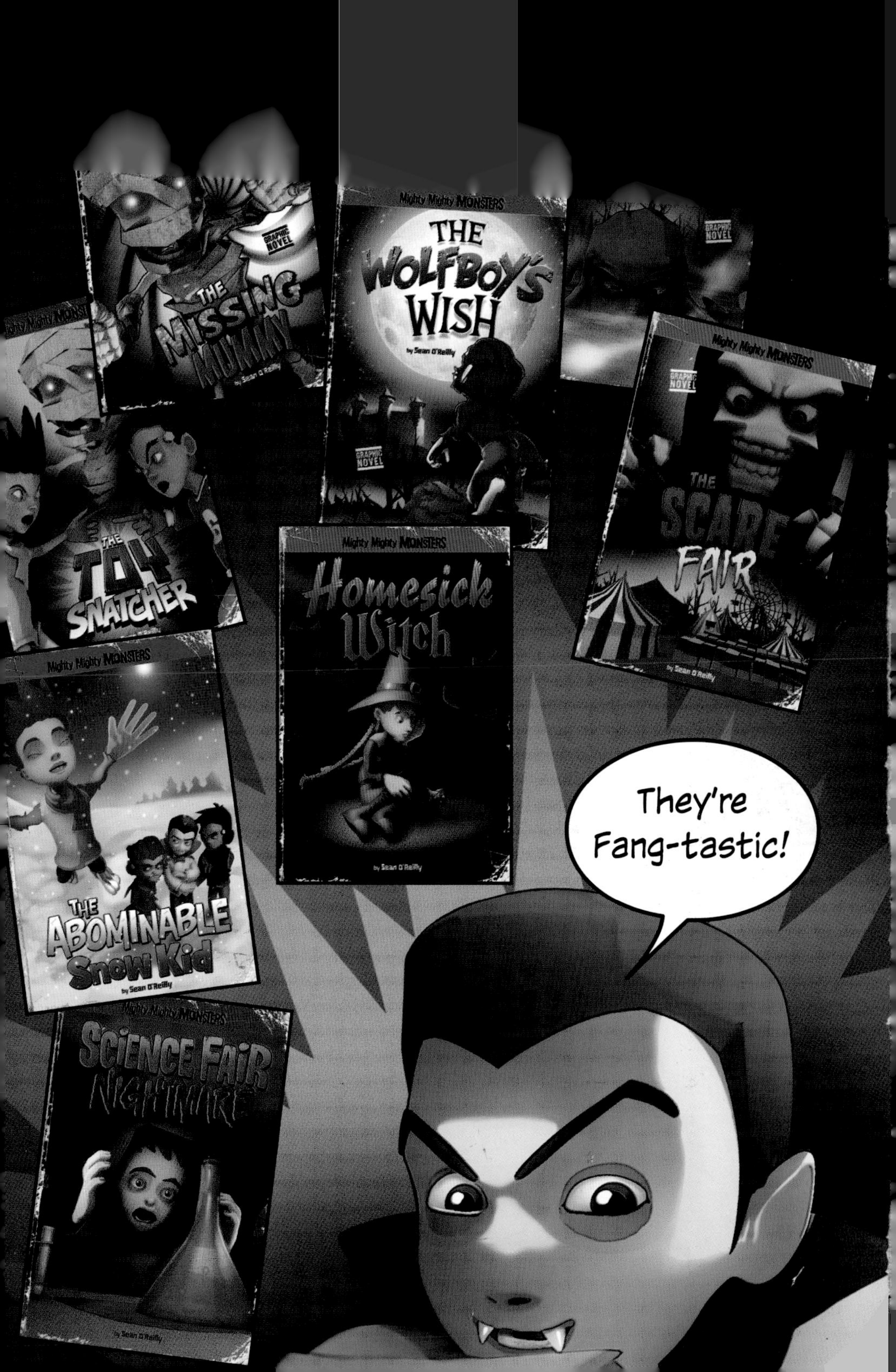

THE MISSING MUMMY
Mighty Mighty MONSTERS
THE WOLFBOY'S WISH
by Sean O'Reilly
THE TOY SNATCHER
Mighty Mighty MONSTERS
Homesick Witch
by Sean O'Reilly
Mighty Mighty MONSTERS
THE SCARE FAIR
by Sean O'Reilly
Mighty Mighty MONSTERS
THE ABOMINABLE Snow Kid
by Sean O'Reilly
Mighty Mighty MONSTERS
SCIENCE FAIR NIGHTMARE
They're Fang-tastic!

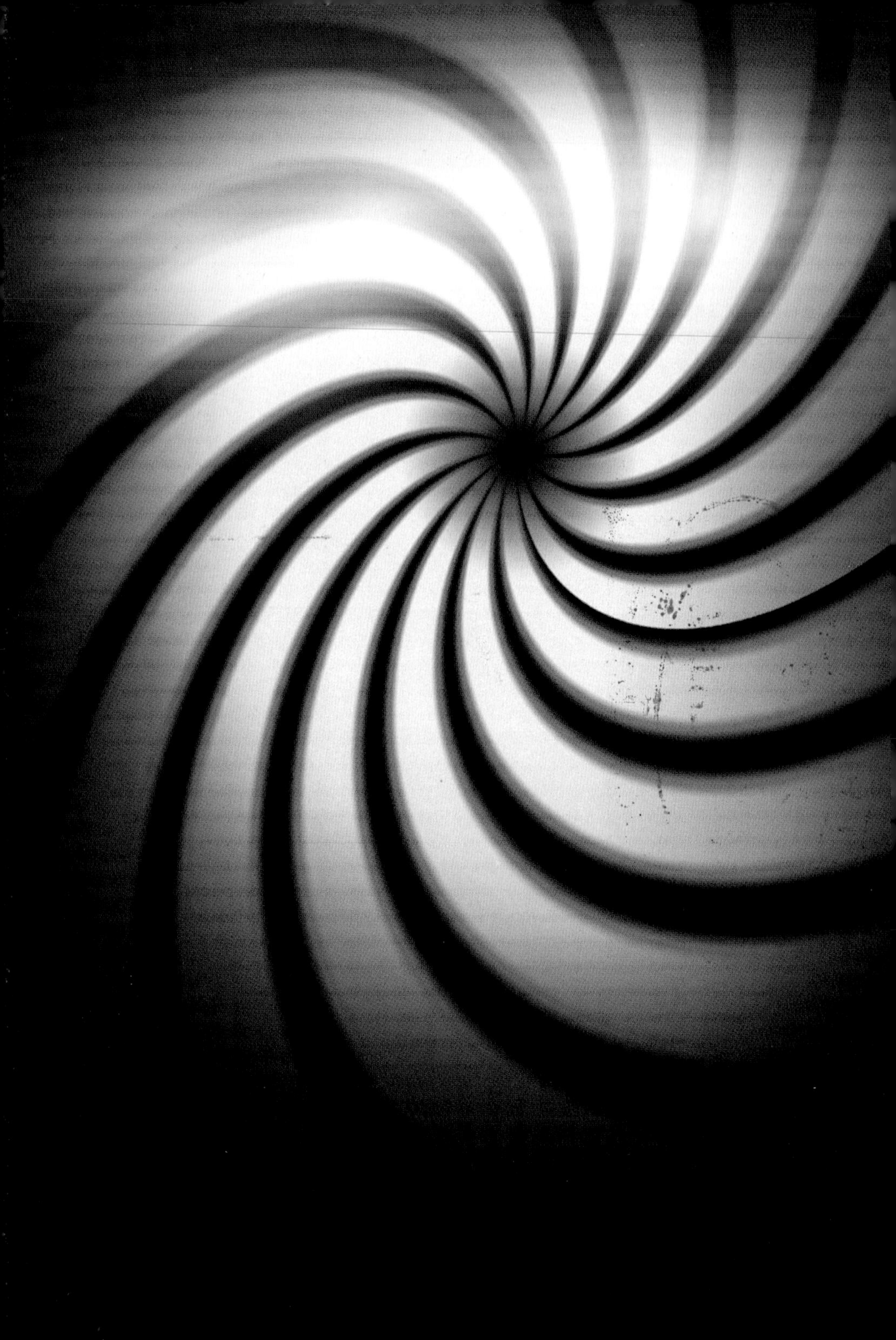

www.raintree.co.uk